Erroneous

Conception

Truth

M.C. CONNER

Printed and bound in the USA

First Printing 2018

Independently published by Matthew Cody Conner

Portland, OR

This book is dedicated to my beautiful wife

and amazing children.

They are my inspiration.

I also want to thank all of the people

in my life that have supported me in this.

M.C. CONNER

"I'm gonna lean up against you,

you just lean right back against me.

This way, we don't have to sleep with our heads in the mud."

- Bubba Blue (Forrest Gump)

Prologue

Erroneous stood in line at the post office looking down at his shuffling feet. He hated lines. The average person would spend five years of their life waiting in line or at a traffic light. It wasn't the time waiting that bothered Erroneous as much as it was standing so close to strangers for that time. He took a long breath in and let it out slowly while he waited for his turn at the counter.

"Next!" The clerk at the counter called.

Erroneous walked up and set his package down on the counter in front of him. The United States Postal Service delivers 493.4 million pieces of mail every day. He waited patiently as the postal worker weighed his package and printed out a label. It took 138 seconds.

"Would you like to add insurance?" The clerk asked.

"Yes." Erroneous declared emphatically.

The package wasn't worth much monetarily, but it was very important to Erroneous that it arrive at the intended destination. He had spent weeks deciding whether to send it at all. He wanted to be confident that all of his deliberation was not for nothing. Erroneous didn`t know if he would have the strength to do it again.

"That will be $21.98." The worker behind the counter informed him.

Erroneous handed over his debit card and the clerk ran it through the register. Afterwards the clerk moved Erroneous' package to a table behind the counter and handed him back his card. Erroneous couldn't help but think of everything that had led to this. He knew his wife would be proud of him.

It was still hard to tell if any of it had been worth it. He may never know, but he would do his part. It was a lot of pain to let go of. Erroneous knew the description was lacking. He wasn't really letting go of the pain. He knew that pain like this wasn't something that ever left. It was something you had to learn to live through. It was just a lot of pain to stop fighting with.

He realized now that people liked to fight with their pain. They liked to hold it close and try to choke the life from it. When you lose some things, you try and keep the pain because it is all you have left of what meant so much. It had taken a while, but Erroneous had discovered that doing that just let the wounding continue.

Erroneous had been through a lot in his life. He had been through some terribly hard things and had to make some very difficult decisions. Sending this package felt like one of the hardest. Part of him wanted to go back and get it, but he didn't. This was the right thing. He needed to do this. He didn't know how the package would be received. It was just something he needed to do for himself.

He imagined what Bella would think about everything that had happened. It didn't seem real most of the time. It seemed like something that had happened to a different person in a different life. Erroneous could almost believe that sometimes, but inevitably something would remind him of the certainty of it all. He knew what Bella would say about it. He could almost hear her laugh as she said it.

"Everyone goes crazy. Sometimes life just hurts too much to process, it's unavoidable. Going crazy is okay, just so long as you make it back."

Erroneous held firmly onto the memory of that laugh.

Chapter 1

"Come dream with me tonight."

-Teddy Ruxpin

Erroneous Conception Truth had already been awake for exactly 378 seconds when he felt his wife touch his shoulder and quietly whisper "Time to get up."

He stopped his count and rolled out of bed. He didn't stretch or yawn, he simply lifted the blankets and with one smooth motion rolled his body into a sitting up position with his feet on the floor. He had been anticipating the movement since shortly after waking and felt a brief surge of satisfaction at the efficiency of it. He touched his phone and the screen lit up displaying the time. It was 4:59 am.

"Only 1 in 5 people are up before 5 am." Erroneous quietly whispered to himself.

He immediately gave himself a mental reprimand for speaking his thoughts out loud. Not only was speaking personal thoughts inefficient but he knew from experience that some people are put off by someone randomly murmuring obscure facts to themselves. Putting people off was something he had learned to avoid at all costs from a very young age.

Erroneous Conception Truth was born on a hippie commune in the California Mountains. Well it may have been a hippie commune at one time, but by the time he was born in the summer of 1980, it was basically a drug house in the woods occupied by runaways. His father was born Frank Oral Gowan. After dropping out of college to become a traveling author and philosopher, he had his name legally changed to Radical Progressive Truth. It was his thought that the name change would help sell his book, The Truth Movement. Rad Truth never finished his book and never travelled. Instead of finding the truth he found drugs.

Erroneous never really knew his mother. His father said she split after the cops raided the commune and shut everything down.

The relationship was never supposed to be serious. Just a couple of free spirits having fun. His father once told him how they did so much acid that summer that Erroneous was almost due before they even knew she was pregnant. Erroneous was an unwelcome surprise and his father was still on his "radical truth" kick. Hence the name Erroneous Conception Truth.

After the commune was shut down, Rad Truth stayed in the mountains and became a meth cook for the local biker gangs. Cooking meth and using meth was Rad Truth's entire life. He seemed to hate his son and could be frequently heard telling his infrequent guests to "ignore the little shit and it would eventually just go away." Whenever Erroneous entered a room that his father was in he was usually met by some sort of thrown object unless the man had succumbed to one intoxication or another.

Erroneous' only valued possession was a Teddy Ruxpin he had gotten when he was 5. Somebody had traded it to his father for meth and he had stolen it a week later after he was sure that Rad Truth had forgotten its existence. Mr. Ruxpin, as he was fond of calling him, had been Erroneous' only teacher growing up and also his only friend. He had learned how to read from the talking bear. At

7 he had memorized all of the books and began creating other tapes

for the bear to play. The tapes were compilations of other people

talking on the radio. He would record phrases in certain orders so

that when played, Mr. Ruxpin would seem to carry on a

conversation. Erroneous would pretend to talk with Mr. Ruxpin,

sometimes for hours at a time.

So Erroneous spent most of his young life reading and

talking to his stuffed bear and hiding out in the old tool shed that

passed for his room. In the evenings he would sneak into the house

and scavenge whatever left over food he could find and fill his

thermos from the tap. By 9 he wasn't even sure that Rad Truth even

remembered that he had a child. Erroneous had taken to exploring

the area surrounding their isolated mountain shanti. He avoided

roads and mostly travelled through the woods.

Nobody had ever been nice to him, so he had an innate fear

of human interaction. He would wander the game trails that ran all

over the mountain. He soon learned that many of them followed a

predictable route that circled close to some of the vacation cabins

that remained empty most of the year. It turns out that the woodland

animals knew the way to every trash can for 20 miles.

Erroneous would sneak into the empty cabins and read. He would read anything they had. Encyclopedias, dictionaries, hunting magazines, reader's digest, he even read the labels on any food or toiletries. When he was most scared, when it was dark and cold in his shed, or he was hiding from his enraged father, Erroneous would quietly whisper interesting facts he had read to Mr. Ruxpin. It made him feel less afraid and alone in those moments.

Erroneous never stole anything. He was afraid people would make it harder to get in if he did and knew his father would take anything of value if found anyway. Sometimes he would watch their TV or listen to the radio, but only for short periods at a time. The distraction made it hard for him to pay attention to anything else going on around him and that made him feel uncomfortable.

He also couldn't help but feel some anxiety every time he saw a lit screen or heard a voice coming from a speaker. His father was fond of watching the TV loudly. He was also fond of arguing with it and punctuating his arguments with violence. A well-founded fear of being hit by a random flying bottle or an intentional kick at 11:30 in the morning, during an episode of All My Children, was a big motivator in his initial decision to move into the tool shed.

Shortly before he turned 14, during his evening trip to the main house for water and table scraps, he found his father dead. Rad Truth was on the sweat stained, pea green couch with several large holes in his chest. His head laid back staring blankly at one corner of the small one room shack.

He could hardly remember his father being anywhere other than that couch. In his eyes it seemed right somehow that it was where he died. Erroneous just stared at his father lying back on the couch for a while. He had no idea how long his father had been dead. He was pretty sure he had been alive the night before, but it could have happened any time after that. He had been out most of the day, and even if it had happened while he was in the shed he probably wouldn't have heard. Even now the TV was on full blast. He imagined there could be a dragon roaring in the room and you wouldn't hear it. He was pretty sure it had been at least a few hours because a large portion of the couch was stained with soaked up blood, but the very far edges seemed to be dry already.

"There were 18,253 gun homicides in America last year." Erroneous whispered to himself.

He turned away from the sight of his father soaking into the couch and switched off the blaring television set. For the first time since entering he took in the rest of the room. It had long been covered in trash and clothes and all manner of other debris, but someone had gone through the effort to throw it all around the room. The kitchen was just another section of the room with a fridge and sink and a small counter that was covered with broken glass and disparate pieces of Rad's meth cooking equipment.

The only other room in the home was the bathroom and it sat with door open and empty except for its usual coating of sludge. He had taken to using the bathrooms in the various cabins he visited or simply using the woods. Both were vastly more sanitary than the pit of disease and infection in his father`s dwelling. He couldn't remember the last time he had been in their bathroom.

Erroneous couldn't quite figure out how to feel. He couldn't say that he loved his father, but Rad Truth was the only other person he knew. His world felt somehow smaller and too big all at the same time. He had never thought about what he would do if his father died. Like any 13 year old, he had never really thought past the day's adventures.

He wasn't sure if he wanted to leave the only place he had ever known, but also wasn't sure if whoever had killed his father would be back. He was sure, whoever the perpetrators were, they had taken anything of value that was easily found. They probably killed Rad thinking he had a big stash of drugs or money somewhere, or maybe Rad had owed them money. Maybe someone had finally just gotten fed up with Rad's big mouth and bad attitude. Erroneous wouldn't have been surprised if it was all three in equal parts.

Eventually his fear of the gunmen returning or being found later by the police overcame his fear of leaving. He went into the kitchen and pulled out the drawer from under the oven. He had to crawl halfway into the hole left behind it, but found his father's secret stash. It was a plastic blue binder that people sometimes used to keep personal documents.

He wasn't surprised to find the small bags of white powder or the aged piece of paper scribbles covering it and titled Recipe. He was however very surprised to find the binder also contained $437 and Erroneous' birth certificate mixed in with the other random papers that Rad had thought important. He removed one threadbare converse and sock, took half the money and his birth certificate and folded them up and tucked them into the sock and put both the shoe and sock back on. It wasn't the most comfortable, but it was the safest place he could think of. The rest of the money he shoved into his pocket as he headed out to his shed.

It had never been much of a room. His bed was a small mattress piled with ratty blankets and located on the plank floor in one corner. He grabbed the small duffle bag that he used to carry things around during his hikes. The zipper was broken but the handles were still good and it held most things just fine.

A wooden work bench was the only other thing in the room beside Erroneous' bed. On top of it was Mr. Ruxpin, his only other pair of jeans and 2 well-worn shirts, as well as a handful of interesting rocks and trinkets he had found during his hikes. He wrapped Mr. Ruxpin along with his tapes in the clothes and crammed the bundle into his bag. He followed those with his thermos. Deciding there was nothing else worth taking he went back to the main house.

He once again surveyed the scene, trying his best to avoid looking directly at his father's body. He had no idea what else he could take with him. He saw a lighter on the table and thought it could come in handy so he picked it up. The numbness had begun to wear off and the mixture of fear and confusion was quickly turning into anger and panic. He could feel tears start to run down his face and blur his sight. He wiped furiously at his eyes and stared down at his father's unmoving boots.

"This is all your fault." Erroneous sobbed down at the dirty leather boots. "You barely gave me anything and now it is gone, and it is ALL YOUR FAULT!"

He was surprised at the volume of his own voice. He still had the lighter in his hand. He reached down and grabbed a piece of paper from the floor. He lit it and softly tossed into another pile of trash next to the couch. He stayed and watched the fire spread from the pile of trash to another pile and run up the curtains. He watched the skirting around the couch begin to curl as the flames licked it and eventually catch fire as well. His face was covered with soot and he was choking on smoke before it became too much and he fled the now burning shack.

Erroneous didn't look back as he ran the mountain trails. He didn't know where he intended to go so he just headed downhill towards the cities and towns he had read about at the bottom of the mountain. It was 1994. He had never been to school and hadn't ever really talked to another person.

Life had thrown Erroneous into the mud since day one, but it was about to kick him full on in the face. Looking back now it was hard for him to even recognize the boy from his memories as the man that he had become. If it hadn't been for his best friend, Dante, that he met shortly after he reached civilization, or his wife who had encouraged him to change his street life ways, Erroneous was sure that his story would have ended a long time ago.

Chapter 2

"Fate is like a strange, unpopular restaurant filled with odd little waiters who bring you things you never asked for and don't always like."

— Lemony Snicket

Erroneous sat on the edge of the bed for another 192 seconds waiting for his wife to finish her hair in the bathroom. Then walked straight from the bed and sat down on the toilet. First thing in the morning is the most popular time to have a bowel movement and the second most frequented bathroom time is right after a person arrives home from work. Also Science has proven that the most efficient position for a bowel movement is leaning forward at a 45 degree angle. He thought to himself as he leaned forward.

After he had finished his morning ablution he stood in front of the mirror and began his daily preparation. The recommended time for brushing your teeth is 2 minutes or 120 seconds. A normal adult has 32 teeth. That provided exactly 3.75 seconds for each tooth or 1.875 seconds for each side of each tooth. Erroneous repeated these pieces of information to himself in his head as he carefully placed the recommended pea sized dab of toothpaste on his brush. He began brushing his teeth while he silently counted to 128 in his head. 128 seconds allowed him to brush each side of each tooth for a full 2 seconds. He had added the 8 seconds because he didn't feel confident in his ability to accurately count to 1.875 and this way he could give each tooth an equal amount of time with confidence.

After brushing his teeth, he shaved. Men spend approximately 3000 hours of their life shaving. Then he got into the shower. He wet his hair, which he buzzed down to exactly ¼ of an inch every Sunday night, then placed a quarter sized amount of shampoo into his hand, rubbed it thoroughly scalp, and began his shower count. From this point his shower would take exactly 5 minutes.

He let the shampoo set in his hair for a 60 count while he scrubbed his hands and then his feet. Then he gave himself another 60 count to rinse the shampoo out of his hair. He then began to methodically wash the rest of his body. His face received a 30 count, he gave his torso 20 seconds and each of his arms and legs 10 seconds. Then he counted 30 seconds for the rinse process.

Afterwards he turned the shower water as hot as he could stand and silently reminded himself that a hot shower can increase oxytocin levels and ease anxiety. He counted to 30 under the hot water then turned it to full cold while reciting in his head that an instant temperature change from hot to cold can relieve fatigue and increase mental alertness. Another 30 count followed while under the cold water. When his count was finished, he turned the water off, stepped out and began to dry himself thoroughly from the head down.

He went back into the bedroom and pulled his work uniform off of the hanger on the back of the door. Each night he washed and ironed his uniform and hung it up for the next morning. Twenty-two percent of men wear a uniform to work. His shoes sat at the foot of the bed with a clean sock neatly placed inside each one.

Erroneous loved that he had a work uniform. He even emulated it during his off days by wearing the same black pants and a plain white or black t-shirt. Not only did it make mornings more efficient and free up mental space to think and make decisions about other things but eliminated many of the variable reactions people can have to one's appearance. He already knew that what he was wearing had been approved by the people he would interact with and that eliminated a layer of anxiety from his every day.

A great amount of Erroneous' day consisted of his internal prompts. His continuous inner dialogue of facts and information, which flowed through his head in reaction to each moment, provided him with a structure for each day. It provided a shield against the overwhelming stimuli of the world around him. Each bit of information helped make the world a little smaller and easier for him to face. Enough information could transform seemed chaos into a natural, logical event or an emotional reaction could be turned into a mindful decision. He was sure that if someone else could peek inside his mind they would think he was insane, but he knew that the unrelenting litany running through his mind was very much the foundation of his sanity.

At 5:15 am He was ready and warming up the car. The average person spends 200 hours per year commuting to and from work. Erroneous knew that translated into 50 minutes per day. He didn't have to be at work until 9 am, but his wife had just started a new schedule that required her to be at work by 6 am.

He didn't mind getting up early and his wife's new shift also came with more hours. He was pleased that they were that much closer to the average median household income of $57,617. When they reached the annual income of $60,195, which his research had shown was the needed amount to live comfortably in Portland, they planned to start a family. It was something that he both wanted and was terrified of. He knew that he no idea how to be a good father and had no role models to build from. He had of course spent an endless amount of time researching the subject, but was deeply afraid that his inability to properly connect with people would handicap him no matter how much information he gathered.

Still, he knew it was important to his wife, Bella. The average childbearing age of an American woman was 28. She was already 36. They probably would have had children already if not for his hang ups. He knew this, and he also knew that the chance of a child being born with Down syndrome increased from 1 in 1,250

when the mother is 20 years old to about 1 in 100 when the mother is

40 years old. While he watched Bella walk from the house to the car,

he weighed having a Down syndrome child or possibly losing Bella

because of waiting, against the perceived challenges of having a

child before being financially ready. While she was getting into the

passenger seat of their green 2003 VW Jetta, he decided that he

would talk to her about trying to have a baby that evening. He was

about to collapse under the anxiety of the decision when she leaned

over and kissed him on the cheek.

"I love you Ron. Ready to go?" she asked.

"I am." He firmly replied and began to back out of the

driveway.

Bella could always calm him with a touch or a word. She

was his anchor and the most genuine, sincere person he had ever

met. She was the only person he had ever trusted completely and the

only person he had ever believed when they told him that they loved

him. To Erroneous, she was the most beautiful person he had ever

seen and he thanked his stars every day that she had settled for him.

Erroneous glanced down at the speedometer to make sure that he was going exactly 35 miles per hour. There are 112,000 people who receive a speeding ticket every day. Speeding is also the second leading cause of accidents and 3,287 people die in a car accident each day. He always went the speed limit. Bella turned on the radio, rolled down the window, and lit a cigarette. She hummed along to the country love song that played through the half blown speakers of the car. Erroneous felt himself try to listen harder and wishing she would hum just a little louder. He loved the sound of her voice. It was that sound that had first pushed him over love's cliff. He was hers the first time he heard it.

They got to the diner, where Bella worked, at 5:42 am. She opened the door and put out her cigarette. "Thank you for driving me so early." She said.

"I don't mind. It is good that you have more hours." He replied.

She leaned over and kissed him on the cheek. "Working more has been good for my figure too. My ring even feels loose, and if you are good later tonight, my clothes might just fall right off." He could feel her breath against his neck. "Have a good day. I love

you." She whispered in his ear.

   He blanked until the sound of the car door closing snapped

him back. "I love you too. Don't let that ring fall off. It's one of a

kind." He called at her back from the open car window as she

walked away. She waved her hand behind her as she dug for

something in her purse. "Or your clothes." He mumbled.

   He waited for her to walk around the end of the building

towards the front doors before turning around and heading towards

the parking lot exit. He had to wait for a young homeless girl to

cross before pulling out into the street. She was wearing a too large,

brown leather jacket with a dingy grey hoodie underneath. She had

the hood pulled halfway over her head and when she looked towards

him he could see her eyes staring out from a dingy face and mass of

unwashed hair. She looked too young to have already lost so much.

   He couldn't help but wonder what had happened in her life to

bring her to where she was. Could it happen to anyone? Could this

girl have been Bella in a different world? According to the last

census there are 4,177 homeless people in the City of Portland.

Erroneous felt a surge of gratitude that he and Bella weren't among them and silently thanked the girl for reminding him of what he had. As he headed to work he felt optimistic and planned the conversation he would have with Bella later about having kids.

Bella was searching through her purse for her work keys when she walked through the door. She could tell from the parking lot that the diner wasn't busy, but she didn't notice the two men standing in front of the counter with guns until one was screaming at her and pushing her down into the booth closest to the entrance. Panic crashed over her in a wave and she could do nothing in the surge except cringe into the corner of the booth.

When the tide of adrenaline and fear lost its edge she was able to slowly make sense of what was happening. She could hear one man in the back yelling at the cook and the other man screaming at the poor girl that served during the graveyard shift as he paced back and forth in front of the diner's main doors. The sour smell of booze and long unwashed human wafted over her strongly every time his steps brought him by the booth in which she cowered.

Bella could hear her coworker sobbing and digging through the drawers at the server station. The man was screaming "Where are the keys! Get me the keys or you are fucking dead!"

It took her a few moments to realize that the girl was searching for a key to the safe. Bella had one on the keyring in her purse. She finally looked up and saw the robber had grabbed the graveyard server by the hair. He was holding the gun to her head while screaming in her face.

"Wait! Wait!" she screamed. "I have a key to the safe. I have a key here in my purse." The man turned towards her and pointedly shook the gun at the crying girls head.

"Then get it!" he yelled. She began to frantically rummage through her purse.

The man had thrown her coworker to the floor and started walking towards her across the diner. Bella's heart was racing and her hands seemed to be ignoring her brain. Finally she felt her grasp close over the bundle of keys. As she pulled them from the purse she heard an explosion.

The sound seemed to push through her body and she instinctively closed her eyes. When she opened them she was once again sitting in the booth. There felt like there was a fire inside her chest and when she reached up to check her hands came away wet and red. She tried to push herself up but slipped on the blood slick

cushions. The effort seemed to drain her of energy.

The man that had been walking toward her, grabbed her

purse and running out the door screamed for the other thug to follow.

The cook ran to call the police and the graveyard server sat sobbing

where she had been tossed. Out of the window next to the booth

Bella could see the sun just breaking over the horizon. The pink light

was mixing with the hazy grey of the Portland morning. She

slumped back in the seat and with a long sigh closed her eyes.

Chapter 3

"Death lies on her, like an untimely frost

Upon the sweetest flower of all the field."

-William Shakespeare

It was 6:03 when Erroneous pulled into the employee parking lot at work. He had an hour before the bakers started and all of the people working in packaging and shipping arrived. Then another hour before the office staff. He worked in janitorial so he came in after everyone started making a mess and stayed later so he could clean up after they left. He didn't mind being early. Approximately 19 percent of workers are late for work once a week and 73 percent of managers don't care. Being early meant he always got the same parking spot he liked and gave him the alone time he needed to indulge in his one true addiction.

He pulled his smartphone out of his pocket. He was always amazed that he had a device in his pocket that allowed him instant access to the cumulative knowledge of all mankind. He was even more amazed and disgusted that most people used it almost exclusively to watch porn and argue with strangers.

The first thing Erroneous did was read the news. He spent the first hour pouring through news feeds. He read the local news and national news and worldwide news. He read conservative media and liberal media and alternative media. He did consider it important to be aware of current events, but the news was also one of his main sources of research prompts.

An article about a man shooting a police officer made him curious about how many police officers are killed each year. There have been 21,541 killed in the line of duty since 1791. That is approximately 95 per year. Then of course he was curious how that compared to civilian deaths. Some research has shown upwards of 14,000 deaths from police interactions between 2000 and 2016. That is more than 875 deaths per year. He continued to follow his prompts and curiosities down a digital rabbit hole of endless information. He was just learning that 17 percent of the population have blue eyes, when his alarm went off.

This alarm was to let him know that he only had half an hour before his shift. He stopped looking up information opened his media app and played the latest song he was trying to learn. Singing is a natural antidepressant, boosts the immune system, increases mental alertness, and even improves posture. While Erroneous knew all of this about singing, none of these were the reasons he sang.

He sang because Bella loved to sing. The first time He saw her she was singing karaoke. He started teaching himself to sing in the hopes that he could impress her. They still went to karaoke together every couple of weeks. Erroneous tried to learn a new song each time.

He sang through the song twice with the music and once by himself to practice. He pictured himself up on the stage singing to Bella while she smiled up at him. Before he had met her, he would never have dreamed of singing in front of anyone, much less a room full of bar patrons. The first time he tried he almost completely panicked. He had looked over towards Bella and found her looking at him. Their eyes met and she nodded encouragingly. He hadn't even spoken with her yet and she was able to erase all of his fear with one look. He knew that moment that he was hooked. Not just on karaoke but on Bella.

After he had finished his 15 minutes of singing practice, he put everything down, lay back against the seat of his car, and began to take long, slow full, breaths. There are many documented benefits of meditation. Mainly, Erroneous had found, that before he had to deal with people it was better to clear his mind and start from a neutral emotional plain.

He opened the car door and stepped out, tucking his phone back into his pocket. He made sure to lock the door. Portland ranked third in the nation for car thefts per capita. He then began the 178 step walk to the building entrance. At step 68 he noticed the police car pull in and park at the curb directly in front of the main doors.

Erroneous wasn't too suspicious. The bread company hired a lot of felons which is how he himself had gotten the job. Every once in a while the police would show for a parole violation or something. He'd once read a study saying that 76% of all inmates end up back in prison within 5 years.

As he entered the building two officers were standing at the reception desk. They looked like your standard boys in blue but there was something different about their demeanor. Most cops he'd met had an air of confidence. Some were nice, most were dicks, but all of them were confident. Neither of these two officers seemed confident. One of them looked very uncomfortable and the other just seemed tired.

Erroneous made sure not to look too long. Sometimes he did that and it had gotten him in trouble with both cops and criminals in the past. Never look more than five seconds, ideally no more than three. Erroneous had learned to see a lot in three seconds.

He started across the small lobby towards the far door marked employees only. He had pushed it halfway open and was about to step through when he heard the all too recognizable sound of somebody trying to read his full name out loud. Even though the words in his name were familiar, people were not familiar with seeing those words as someone's name. This always caused them to look past the words and just assume the name was foreign, which inevitably led to an awkward Spanish accent and a poor attempt at rolling 'r' sounds.

Erroneous didn't immediately turn around. He stepped through the door and let it close behind him. He knew that the officers were looking for him, but needed a second to think about why before he actually faced them. He did not like the police and was especially wary of them showing up unexpected. Police only show up when something bad has happened and their main job is to find someone to blame for whatever that was. Erroneous had learned that it is best to be as ready as possible before talking to the cops.

He ran a mental checklist and concluded that he had not missed any scheduled appointments with his PO and was not behind on any fines. Any surprise check in would have been done by his regular parole officer. The only other thing he could think was that something had happened with Bella or Dante. He dug his phone out of his pocket and dialed the diner. After 5 rings, the answering machine picked up. He ended the call and immediately pressed redial. The same robotic female voice answered after 5 rings instructing him to leave a message and someone would return their call when they were not busy with another customer.

He was getting ready to try again when the door swung open and Gina from reception stepped through. She jumped slightly to find Erroneous suddenly standing next to her.

"Oh! Ron, I thought I had seen you come in." She said recovering herself. "There are a couple police officers here to speak with you. They are waiting in the lobby."

"They're here for me?" He replied. "Um, ok. I will be right out."

"I will let them know." She turned and went right back through the door.

Erroneous called the diner again and once again the machine picked up. With a sigh he turned and went back through the door to the lobby and the awaiting officers. Both officers turned towards him as he entered the room. Erroneous immediately noticed something different about the way they looked at him.

Usually when a police officer looks at you there is a calculation that you can almost feel. They seem to constantly be looking for that small movement that might signify danger or a lie. There is always that glint of suspicion and that slight grimace as if they can taste the grains of salt that they take with your every word.

These officers didn't have any of these things showing in their eyes or on their faces as they watched Erroneous walk across the lobby towards them. If anything they looked nervous and guilty. A few steps away he met each of their gazes.

The officer on the right was slightly shorter and stockier than his partner. He had the look of someone that always scowled. As Erroneous met his eyes what he saw there took all of the weight away from that scowl. The officer could only meet his eyes for a heartbeat before turning his whole body away and looking towards the cruiser parked outside at the curb. When Erroneous switched his gaze to meet the eyes of the taller officer on the right his dread deepened. The second officer did not turn away from the eye contact like his partner. The man seemed to visibly collapse in on himself as Erroneous drew within a couple steps and stopped in front of him.

"Gina said you officers needed to speak with me?" He asked. "What can I do for you?"

There was a heavy, awkward pause as the shorter officer turned and briefly shared a meaningful look with his partner then turned his gaze purposefully back towards the police car outside. It was obvious that whatever was happening, this officer would rather be anywhere else. Erroneous could feel the unease rolling off of the two men and could feel it building in himself as a result.

"Uh uhm. Hrmm." The taller officer cleared his throat twice making Erroneous think that whatever he was about to say was so difficult he was having trouble getting it out.

"Are you Erroneous Conception Truth?" He asked, once again adding a slight Spanish pronunciation to his name.

"Most people just call me Ron." Erroneous replied. "It is easier."

"Right. Uh uhm, Ron." The officer continued. "Are you the husband of a Bella Truth?"

Erroneous felt himself cringe inside at the question. "Yes. Is everything okay?"

"Mr. Truth, the diner your wife worked at was robbed this morning." The officer began, but Erroneous noticed the past tense used by the officer and cut him off.

"What do you mean worked? What has happened?" Erroneous asked, but knew inside what had happened. He could feel it. He asked hoping that the officer would give him any other answer except the one he knew he was about to get. He could feel his heart beating faster and the start of a cold sweat. The officer stared at him

for a second before answering. He had the look of a man about to

kill a loved family pet because it was sick.

"During the robbery, hmm hrmm, your wife was shot. She

uh died on the scene." The words seemed to leave the man an empty

husk.

Erroneous felt the words hit him. It wasn't like getting hit in

the gut. It was more like falling out of a tree onto your back and

having everything knocked out of you. It seemed like an eternity

before he took a breath. The shock of it numbed him and seemed to

set him on fire at the same time.

There were 15,549 gun deaths in the US last year. He could

almost feel the thought push into his stomach and catch on fire. His

breath quickened as the pressure built inside and outside, like he was

being crushed from both directions. Erroneous barely noticed that

the officer was still talking.

"Sir, we need you to come identify the body and fill out some

paperwork for its release." Erroneous heard him say through the

haze. He couldn't find his voice so he just nodded his head yes.

"We can give you a ride." The officer offered.

"That's okay. I can take myself." Erroneous heard himself reply from what seemed like the bottom of hole.

"Please take your time and if you need anything you can call this number." The officer was pressing a card into his hand while his stockier counterpart had already started escaping towards the exit. Erroneous simply nodded again and watched as the officers got into their car and pulled away.

Erroneous could hear the receptionist Gina talking to him but couldn't make sense of it. He didn't care to try. He could feel everything closing in on him. There was almost a sense of awe at how easily the importance of everything could be simply wiped away.

"Please tell Dave that I am sorry but I need the day off. Actually just tell him that I quit."

Erroneous didn't wait for a response, just simply left the building and began walking back to his car.

He didn't know why he quit other than he just couldn't think of a reason to work there or anywhere anymore. As he thought about it he struggled to find any reasons at all. He must have blanked the walk to his car because the next thing he knew he was sitting in the driver seat staring through the windshield at nothing. He didn't

know how long he had been there, but it had to have been several

minutes because the vehicle was running and the temperature gauge

showed that the engine was already reading warm.

He didn't trust himself to drive right this second so he turned

the car off, pulled the keys out of the ignition and dropped them in

the passenger seat. He needed to think but couldn't. He needed to

breath but couldn't. His world had caved in burying him alive,

suffocating him and he could feel the pain and panic filling

everything, growing and pushing itself out of him. He crumpled in

upon himself as sobs began to wrack his body. The first tear burned

down his cheek like acid.

Chapter 4

"The only way to have a friend is to be one."

-Ralph Waldo Emerson

Dante awoke to the sound of fighting. He sat up quickly, feeling his face peel off the armrest of his leather couch. The sound of crashing and screams were quieter than they should be and he realized he had fallen asleep with the TV still on. Dante loved Kung Fu movies, especially the old movies from the 60's, 70's and 80's.

Not just the Bruce Lee movies that every poser knows either. He was proud of his collection which included classics like the Five Venoms and Fist of Fury, but also had some of the more sought after obscure films like House of Traps and Lady Whirlwind. Other people put on nature and storm sounds to fall asleep. Dante passed out on his couch every night to the sounds of Bruce Lee, Jackie Chan, and Yuen Biao kicking ass.

He left the TV on as he got up and walked into the kitchen of his downtown studio apartment. He was still wearing his clothes from the day before, but he almost always woke up in his clothes from the day before. Dante could never see the point of wasting money on things like pajamas. He lived alone so there were no other fragile sensibilities to offend. If he was going to change into anything before bed it would be into nothing. When he did have someone staying over it was usually more of a reason to skip right to being naked and with any luck stay that way well into the next day.

He popped a single serve cup into his coffee machine, slid his coffee mug under the spout and pressed the button for 8 ounces. He leaned against the counter and watched as coffee begin to spurt into his cup. The mug was heat sensitive and he loved watching the Marijuana leaf on it appear as if by magic as it filled with hot coffee every morning. When it finished he mixed in some sugar and the powder creamer he kept on the counter. He walked back over to the couch with his coffee and set it down on the table to cool a little while.

Dante picked a small glass jar up off the coffee table and pulled the cork from the top. Holding the jar opening beneath his nose, Dante breathed in deeply. He held the breath for a long moment letting the tangy fruity smell of the flowers inside fully absorb into his nose and mouth. He carefully pulled one of the dense buds out of the jar and began breaking it apart. The trichomes were so thick it looked like the weed had been coated in sugar. Dante rubbed his fingers together enjoying the tackiness the sticky weed left on the tips. He then packed the bowl the two foot bong that lived on his coffee table.

He had to dig deep into the couch cushions to find a lighter. Pulling one of what he was sure was many lost lighters from the abyss, he flicked the flame alive and touched it to the crystally green in the bowl. He watched the glass chamber become thick and milky with smoke before pulling the carb and inhaling deeply to clear the bong. His deep inhale was reflexively followed by a hard coughing exhalation. After his coughing fit had passed, Dante picked up his cup of coffee and leaned back into the couch sipping as his favorite hazy feeling began to creep over him.

This was his favorite strain. He and E grew it themselves and had named it Blueberry Muffins. It used to be their biggest money maker before weed started to become legal. After that it became too hard for small time freelance business men to make any kind of living on growing. Now they just grew for personal and Dante made his living in real estate.

Dante didn't love selling houses and definitely didn't have the work ethic or drive to turn his broker's license into millions. It was originally Erroneous' idea, but it fit Dante's lifestyle pretty well. He got to work for himself so he could sleep in or get off early. There was rarely anyone except the occasional bank or client to look over his shoulder and make sure he was working.

Dante didn't do well with structure or authority. He wanted to feel like he had the freedom to stop doing whatever he was doing right then and smoke a bowl, or to tell some asshat that he was an asshat. With this job he could do that without having to worry about some micromanaging boss giving him a pink slip. He had no wife and no kids so as long as he sold a few houses a year he was able to clear rent, groceries, and still have enough after bills to cover bar nights.

Dante liked things crude and simple. He had no illusions about his self-centeredness. He quite simply just didn't like people and if it didn't get him paid, laid, or high he really didn't have any time for it. A court appointed counselor had once told him that he had major trust issues. Every woman he had a more than a two week relationship with seemed to strongly agree. There were only two people in the world Dante trusted or cared about. The first was himself. The other was Erroneous.

Dante and Erroneous were just two lost kids when they met over 20 years ago. Neither one of them had anybody in the world at the time. Maybe it was the fact that they both were completely alone in the world that had caused them to bond so strongly from the start, but they had had each other's back since day one.

He was almost 16 years old and serving the last half of a 1 year stretch in juvie when he first met E. Dante had been caught selling weed at school. It probably wasn't the weed that got him pinned with a full 12 months. The fact that he was already on probation for the same thing and a school security officer had broken his arm falling down some stairs while Dante was trying to get away was probably what really did it. That had persuaded the prosecution to lay an assault charge on him as well and voila, a full year's vacation at camp get right.

When Erroneous first entered C pod at Placer County Juvenile Detention Center, Dante had never seen someone that looked less like they belonged in jail. There was a certain amount of anger and aggression that hung like a natural cologne on most of the people you saw inside. They had a skulk or swagger. There was a danger to their presence.

It was the bearing of a predator and Erroneous did not have it. There was no meanness to the kid. In most circles that might be a compliment, but in this particular social environment it was an invitation for abuse. There is no honor among criminals, no sense of social justice. They have no desire for unnecessary challenges or the sense of accomplishment that comes with them. An easy target like Erroneous was a free lunch.

Dante watched as the guards walked the new arrival to the last empty cell in C pod. Just like the rest of the pod's current occupants, Dante crowded into the common area to get a look at the new member of their little delinquent community. It was obvious that this kid hadn't even received the most basic of how to survive in jail lesson,s because he made eye contact with each of the boys in the pod as he passed.

Dante couldn't even count how many times he had heard someone in a movie say, "Whatever you do, don't look them in the eye."

Dante noticed the face of each boy change from hard to slightly surprised to nearly murderous and felt his pity for the kid grow even more. He was even more taken aback when that gaze finally locked with his own eyes. It wasn't the calm or angry stare, meant to intimidate that you usually received in this environment. It also didn't contain any of the fear or confusion that one might expect. There was a calm, searching, quality to the boy's eyes. It was only there for a moment and then quickly replaced by the look of someone who had figured out whatever they were looking at.

Dante had been looked at by a lot of people in a lot of different ways, but there was something about the way this kid looked at you. The way he looked at you made you feel seen. There was something about the change in his eyes. That light of revelation that glimmered out made you feel like he saw more about you than you wanted him to. You felt like he was looking at you naked. It made you feel exposed and vulnerable. No wonder everyone seemed to react to the breach in etiquette with even more venom than usual.

51

The guards stood by the door of the cell as he entered, lay the standard issue pile of sheets, blankets, and jail scrubs on the short metal framed bed and sat down next to them. Then the guards simply turned and walked out of C pod leaving the new addition to his fate. Dante watched as the main pod bully, Alastor, immediately started to whisperingly confer with a couple of his cronies. Their looks over towards the newly occupied cell made their intentions so clear it was almost comical.

After they finished with their hushed exchange, Alastor and his main goon Lance began to saunter towards the newly occupied cell. They were members of the same gang. Dante couldn't remember what they called themselves, but he was sure it started with a street name and ended with killers or something just as cliché.

Dante had never had the inclination to join any of the gangs in his neighborhood. He didn't consider himself the same kind of criminal as guys like Alastor and Lance. His last foster home wasn't big on things like shoes and clothes that fit and didn't have holes. There weren't a lot of job opportunities for underage poor kids in his neighborhood, so Dante sold weed to the kids at his school. Guys like Alastor enjoyed hurting people. They had no problem selling crack to their cousin or shooting up a corner store because the owner had called the cops last time they had tried to rob it. Dante wanted no part of shit like that.

Dante's parents both went to prison when he was a baby and he was raised by his grandfather until he was 9. When he was 8 he had gotten into trouble for picking on another kid. Some older kids had goaded him into it by calling him a pussy and chicken. He realized now that the assholes had just wanted to see a couple little kids fight. He will never forget what his grandfather told him that day.

"Dante, do you know why it ain't no good to be a bully and hurt people with no reason?" He had asked.

"I know it's bad grandpa." He had answered hoping to skip a lecture.

His grandfather persisted, as he always did. "There's already little enough peace and joy in this life without throwing any away. Being a bully or being in one of these gangs is angry, hurtful business. It's awful hard to find joy and be so angry, and hard to find any peace while making so many enemies."

Dante's grandfather always could show you the sense in making the right decision. He died the next year and Dante had been in the system ever since. He had found himself plenty of trouble, but had stayed out of the gangs and violence. Maybe not everybody agreed with him, but Dante knew there was a difference between being a bad person and just being on the wrong side of the law.

Alastor had reached the cell and stood just inside the entrance with Lance leaning menacingly against the door frame. "Why you lookin so hard at me back there punk? You think I'm pretty? Wanna be my bitch?" Alastor asked the new kid loud enough that he could be sure everyone in the pod heard him.

Lance snickered behind him. Some people just can't feel important unless everyone is looking at them and Alastor was one of those people. Everything had to be a show. Dante found it more than a little pathetic.

The new kid didn't answer. He just quietly stood up, walked around Alastor, and calmly pushed through Lance on the way out of his cell. Lance and Alastor shared a look of confusion as the kid walked over to the table containing the cell's shared collection of books and board games. He picked up a thick reader's digest, sat down and began to flip through the pages. Alastor and Lance followed him over and stood over top of him staring down.

"Hey! I'm talking to you!" Alastor said loudly down at the sitting boy. "You fucking deaf?!"

The kid didn't even look up, just kept flipping through pages. Maybe he knew, like everyone else, that there was no right thing to say to a guy like Alastor in a situation like this. It was Lance that swung first, hitting the kid in back of the shoulder as he turned away from the blow.

Alastor immediately followed, raining punches of his own down on the boy. Dante noticed with more than a little admiration that the kid sure knew how to take a beating. He had curled and tucked the right side of his body up against the table where he was sitting and was using his left arm to cover his left side. Dante watched as he would turn ever so slightly as blows landed causing them glance off without as much impact.

Dante winced slightly at the sight. Not because it seemed like the punches hurt, but because he knew there were no easy ways to learn how to get beat like that. Dante's grandfather had been a boxer. It had been the punches that had taken his life even though it wasn't until years after they had stopped landing. He had loved to talk to Dante about what made a great fighter.

He once said, "Some people think strength and speed are what wins fights. They do play their part, but in a real fight, when both opponents are trained and skilled and determined, it is toughness that decides the outcome more often than not. You can't always avoid getting hit and life isn't always gonna let you fight back. How far you get in this life is decided less by how hard a punch you can give and more by how hard a punch you can take."

Dante had to admit to being pleasantly surprised at the unexpected toughness from this new kid. He was becoming more intrigued by the moment. Even so, nobody could take punches forever and he hoped the guards showed to break it up before the boy got hurt too bad. He was just about to go over and stop it himself when something happened that nobody expected.

The new kid stomped down hard on Alastor's foot making him take a step back. The boy took the opportunity to stand and swing with the hand still holding the thick copy of Reader's Digest. The hard spine of the book made a solid thump against the side of Alastor's head.

He dropped like a sack of dirt. It was so sudden that the entire pod seemed to freeze. The shouting of entertained witnesses stopped. It seemed the only sound was the hard breathing of the boy standing there with a book in his hand and surveying the gathered stares for any further attacks.

Lance appeared unwilling to continue the altercation with Alastor holding his head and groaning on the ground. He held his hands up, the universal sign for I'm done, and went over to help his partner deal with his wounded face and pride. The boy waited, watching intently as Lance helped Alastor up and walked him over to his cell. When it appeared that they had retreated officially, at least for now, he just sat back down and started flipping pages in the book again.

Dante had never seen anything like it and almost let out a cheer for the kid. Watching that quiet kid knock Alastor into yesterday was the most entertaining thing he had witnessed since being there. Everybody loves an underdog but in the real world the underdog doesn't win. In real life the big dogs and the bad guys win. Dante wasn't sure how much faith he had left in the world but watching the right person win, even if it was just this once, gave him a little more.

He walked over and sat down at the bench across the table from the boy. "I'm not much for reading, but you just made me a huge fan of books." He said.

"I like reading." The boy replied in a quiet straight forward way without looking up.

"Yeah, I bet." Dante continued. "You know that Alastor asshole will probably be back for more. Guys like him aren't known for letting things go."

The kid just nodded and kept reading. "What are you in for?" Dante pressed

"Arson. I lit my house on fire. They thought I killed my dad too, but I didn't." The kid answered in his calm matter of fact way.

"Holy shit! You must be fucked up in the head right now!" Dante exclaimed.

The new kid didn't respond. "You drink?" Dante asked trying to keep the conversation going. "I have some pruno that I made. Come on, nobody will fuck with you in my cell and we can have a drink to celebrate your first day in." Dante invited with a

sarcastic chuckle, pushing himself up and away from the table.

The kid didn't laugh with him, still too new Dante guessed.

He could probably still feel all the places he had just been hit. Even

so he did get up and follow. Dante led him to the cell he called

home.

"Have a seat." Dante gestured towards his bunk as he opened

his foot locker.

He began to carefully remove the extra blankets and cloths he

had concealing the bags of fermenting fruit he kept in the bottom.

The hardest part of making prison wine was not getting caught by

the guards. He had already lost a batch to a cell sweep. He was pretty

sure Alastor had ratted him out. He looked up to find the kid staring

at him intently.

"You can't look at people like that. They don't like it,

especially not in here. Hasn't anyone told you that before?" Dante

asked.

"I know. I can't help it sometimes." The kid answered.

"Well you should help it before somebody like Alastor tries to help it for you again." Dante said pulling out the Ziploc bag he had been looking for.

"This stuff tastes like a dog's butthole, but it will fuck you up." He said as he opened the bag and poured some of the sour smelling liquid into a cup.

He handed the cup to the kid and watched as he took a small sniff and made a face. Dante didn't blame him. He wasn't exactly a brew master. People still drank every drop. At the end of the day there were only a couple ways to make being imprisoned better. Getting wasted on homemade gut rot and doing whatever drugs somebody smuggled in their colon were basically at the top of the list.

"Come on don't be afraid, it won't kill you. Bottoms up." Dante prompted.

The boy grimaced and took a large swallow. His face twisted up and he immediately started choking and coughing. Dante couldn't help but laugh some as he stood up and pounded the kid on the back. It was definitely an acquired taste.

"It's alright, you'll be okay, just catch your breath." He encouraged.

"Why is it so bad? What's in it?" The kid asked him when his body finally stopped trying to reject the foul concoction. His eyes and nose were still running and his voice sounded a little harsh.

Dante couldn't help but feel a little slighted. "Mashed oranges, sugar, ketchup, you know the usual stuff you make pruno out of. It took me weeks to make. It's not that bad. You think you could do better?" Dante asked a little defensively.

"I don't know. I read a book about it once. It shouldn't take as long to make if you add bread for yeast. I don't think you have to put so much stuff in it either. You just need sugar and yeast to make alcohol." The boy informed him. There was no criticism or pride in the kid's voice just a calm statement of information.

Some people might have taken the boys words as an insult to their pride but not Dante. Dante only made the wine for two reasons. The first was because it was boring here and getting drunk made the time go by faster. The second was because someday soon he would be let out of here and get put back in some shit hole foster house. He was hoping that he could get enough money on his books so that

when he got out he would have a stash to run away on.

"So, you're telling me that you can help me make this hooch

better and faster?" Dante asked the kid, more than a little interested.

"I guess." The kid answered.

"I think I am going to like you kid, what's your name?"

Dante asked next.

"Erroneous Conception Truth." The boy responded.

"Err…, what the fuck? Never mind. What does it start with?"

Dante asked.

"An E." Erroneous replied.

"Great! Fuck that other mess. I am going to call you E."

Dante told him. "That good with you E?"

"I think I like it better like that anyway." Erroneous agreed.

"Alright E. If you help me make this shit better and faster, I

will help you keep dickhead Alastor off your back. Deal?" Dante

offered holding out his hand towards Erroneous.

"Deal." Erroneous agreed taking his hand and giving it a firm

shake.

As far as Dante was concerned that ended up being the best deal he had ever made. Erroneous had never stopped helping Dante do things better and faster. Dante had never stopped looking out for E. It was important to have someone you can count on.

He could feel the munchies kicking in. If he timed it right he could grab a couple monster breakfast burritos and meet E at work on his first break. He grabbed his phone off the coffee table and swiped the screen alive. He had somehow missed two calls from E already. He must have been sleeping well. There wasn't a voicemail, but that wasn't surprising. E never left voicemails. He once told Dante that he didn't like saying things to people when he couldn't see or hear how they were reacting to them.

He pulled up his tracking app. Dante and E had been on the same phone plan ever since they could afford to have phones. He knew it might be a little much, but he was very protective of Erroneous and probably checked on the little dot that represented E's location at least ten times a day. It made him feel better to know where E was when He couldn't be around. Bella gave him the hardest time about it. She was constantly reminding him the E was hers and Dante would have to find someone for himself someday.

The little dot was not where it was supposed to be. It should be sitting safely at E's place of work, but it wasn't. Dante had known E for a long time. Some people take random days off of work. E did not. Some people loved the unexpected and to be spontaneous. E did not.

Erroneous thrived on structure and routine. He liked to be in the same places and doing the same things. As soon as Dante saw that little dot moving, he knew something was wrong. He tapped E's number and the little green phone symbol and listened to the digital ring as he waited for E to pick up.

"Dante?" There was something in E's voice Dante had never heard before.

"What's wrong man? Why aren't you at work?" Dante asked, more than a little worried at this point.

"They killed her Dante. They killed her. They killed her." E just kept repeating it in a broken voice.

"Wait. Killed who? What the fuck is going on E?" Dante was starting to panic.

"They shot Bella. She's dead. I am going to see her. I have to go Dante. They killed her." Erroneous hung up.

"Fuck fuck fuck fuck. What the Fuck?!" Dante didn't even bother to change out of yesterday's clothes before grabbing his keys and running out the door.

He didn't stop to lock the door behind him and he didn't return the greeting of the neighbor he passed in the building lobby as he rushed through. Erroneous was more to Dante than just a friend. E was his brother and the person he cared most about in the world, maybe the only person he cared about in the world. All that mattered right now was that E needed him so Dante would be there.

Chapter 5

"It's so much darker when a light goes out than it would have been if

it had never shone."

— John Steinbeck

Erroneous had been sitting outside of the medical examiner's office for 1028 seconds when Dante called. It had taken him longer to get there than it should have, but he had stopped twice to call Dante. Cell phone use while driving leads to over 1.6 million crashes per year. He had also stopped one other time just to catch his breath.

His emotions burned through him like waves of wildfire. One moment he could feel the pain and panic rising like a physical thing. In the next it had passed leaving only ash and numbness in its wake. Then the heat would begin to build again.

The whole world seemed much bigger than it was just a couple hours earlier. It was too big, or maybe he was too small now that he had lost something so important. The sounds were too loud, the light was too bright, and everything was moving too fast. It was as if all of the sudden he could feel the world spinning underneath him.

He squeezed his eyes shut pressing his palms into the sockets. He rubbed them vigorously like it could clear this day from his sight. He wished that when they opened again he would find himself just waking to the sounds of Bella getting ready for work. The sounds of cars and people passing just seemed to grow louder.

He opened his eyes and stared blankly at the building. He expected it to look more like a police station from the movies. Instead it just looked like an office building. Squeezing his eyes closed again he tried to calm himself with long deep breaths. Knowing what waited inside, Erroneous felt like it should be dark and rainy outside the building. There should be thunder and lightning and foreboding music.

When he cracked his eyes again the sun was still shining brightly and the sounds of traffic and people were still too loud and energetic. He waited for shock and numbness to pass over him again and took one more deep breath. Then he got out of the car and started walking towards the building. He didn't bother to lock the door.

The thought went through his head and he started to turn and go back but stopped. Usually it was something he would have had to do, knowing that the unresolved detail would rattle around in his head causing distraction and anxiety. There were approximately 6000 auto thefts in Portland last year. Right now it seemed too insignificant to matter. He had already lost what was really important. They could have the car if they wanted.

There was a sitting area on his right and a large reception desk on his left when he walked through the double glass doors into the building. He walked over to the desk and was greeted by a very business-like lady. Her smart skirt suit was dark and the blouse beneath the jacket was a nondescript cream color.

"How can I help you?" She asked.

She was formal but polite. It looked like she had been doing the job for 20 years and never had a good day at work. Erroneous wasn't sure what to say so he just dug the card the officer had given him out of his pocket. On it was the address and phone number for the examiners office along with a case number. He looked at it for a moment then handed it over the desk to the waiting receptionist.

She let out a long quiet sigh through her nose as she took the card. He watched as the corner of her mouth turned down slightly as she set it down in front of her keyboard and entered something in the computer. He imagined that every time she saw one of the small cards she was hoping that maybe this one time it wouldn't be the same as the others. There were 36,640 deaths last year in the state of Oregon. He wondered if they all had a little card and felt bad for the lady behind the desk.

"If you could just wait over there, someone will be with you shortly." She said handing back the little card and gesturing towards the sitting area across the room.

He stared at the card for few more moments then shoved it back into his pocket. He walked over and sat down in the closest chair. There was no one else waiting. Erroneous wasn't sure exactly what to do.

It was hard to look at anything. He couldn't quite put his finger on why. Nothing looked any different than before, it just felt different when he saw it. There the carpet was, just sitting there gray and getting walked on like any other day. There the chair was, just sitting there getting sat on like any other day. There were the plants growing in their pots and the doors opening and closing and the cars driving by just like any other day. Everything was just fulfilling its purpose the same way it did any other day.

On any other day that is probably what Erroneous would have seen when looking at all of these things. He would even have found some comfort and satisfaction in the mundane consistency of it all. Now it just seemed pointless. He even felt angry that it was all still there just like any other day. It felt unfair that he could lose everything, could lose his purpose, and all of these things that didn't matter would get to keep theirs.

It was too much just sitting there so he got up and started slowly pacing around the waiting area. Americans spend 13 hours sitting and only walk approximately 2.5 miles during the average day. The fact ran through his head. Usually his mind grabbed onto each little fact, standing on them like firm little islands in the chaos. They would help him put everything in place, but now they seemed to keep slipping away like the hands of his mind were covered in oil.

He could feel the pressure start to build. He sat back down and just tried to concentrate on breathing.

Several minutes passed before a lady very similar to the one seated behind the reception walked through a door on the wall. She wore a similar dark suit and light blouse and also seemed to carry the same weight of working in a place such as this for too long. She scanned the almost empty room briefly and upon seeing Erroneous began to approach.

He stood up and self-consciously straightened his shirt as if in doing so it would somehow hide the dishevelment he felt inside. As she got closer he could see that this lady had a softness to her mannerisms that the receptionist lacked and a lot more pity in her eyes. He decided that he liked the receptionist more. The pitying look just made him feel like a broken person. It just reminded him that everything was broken.

Erroneous pulled the card back out of his pocket and held it ready hoping she would ask for it. He wanted her to take it and stop looking at him. People only look at you like that when what is, broken can't be fixed. He wanted to be a case number, just business, not a broken person. He wanted to be anything other than the reflection he saw in the woman's soft sympathetic eyes.

"Mr. Truth?" She said questioningly and holding out her hand.

"Used to be." Erroneous thought to himself.

"Yes." He answered pressing the card into her outstretched hand.

"My name is Angel Breen. I am a grief counselor with the State of Oregon. How are you doing so far?" She continued as she took the card and slid it into the clipboard she was carrying.

"The world has ended but doesn't have the sense to know it." He thought.

"Fine." He answered flatly.

"I want you to know that we are here to help in any way that we can." She replied in an overly comforting voice. "I am going to need to see your ID for verification purposes and then we can go from there."

Erroneous pulled out his wallet and opened it to retrieve his driver's license. He froze for a long moment as he saw a picture of him, Bella, and Dante that he kept in the clear plastic cover right inside. All of them were laughing in the photo. He remembered that night.

They had all gone out drinking together. Portland had the fifth most bars per capita of any major US city at 13.3 per 100,000 people. It was Bella's idea to cram into one of those little picture booths and Dante had told the joke. Erroneous could still hear Dante telling the joke.

"One guy says to another guy, I just saw a man-eating shark at the aquarium." He remembered Dante saying with them all crammed tight into the small booth. "The other replied, so what, I just saw a man eating pussy at the strip club."

Erroneous had laughed so hard that they had all almost fallen out of the photo booth. He loved jokes that played on words and Dante's crude delivery only made it funnier in his opinion. Bella had made him put the picture in his wallet. She told him that he didn't laugh enough and that it was supposed to remind him to do so more often.

It was definitely one of his favorite memories and whenever he looked at it he had felt happy. Everytime except now. Now the happy ran into the pain and everything in his head began to spin. He felt his eyes begin to burn. He took a big swallow, removed his ID, handed it over quickly then folded his wallet with the picture inside and crammed it into his pocket. He only wished the pocket was deeper so he could push the picture farther away.

"Thank you." She glanced at his ID and handed it back. "Just follow me right this way."

He slid the license into his front pocket not wanting to face the picture again so soon and followed her back through the door in the wall. He found himself in a hallway lined with doors. She led him to the third on the right and held the door open for him as he walked in. The room was barely bigger than a closet and contained only a small table and two basic metal chairs on either side.

Angel gestured for him to sit down across the table as she took the seat closest to the door. He sat down at the table and clasped his hands in front of him. The room wasn't what he had expected. On TV they always take you into a pale, blue green lit morgue with dead people on tables. There is always some pasty skinned medical examiner making inappropriate dead people jokes and a hard ass detective acting grumpy that he hadn't solved the case yet.

"Where's her body?" Erroneous asked Angel. "When will I get to see her?"

"I understand this is a little overwhelming. Your wife's body is being held at the morgue as part of an active investigation." Angel began informing him. "When the investigation is over the body will be released to you."

Erroneous just nodded and continued to stare at his hands as they clasped and unclasped over and over. He felt like he should say something or ask a question but couldn't. He was having trouble fighting off the urge to stand up and run out of the building. He wasn't sure if things being less like the movies was making it easier or more difficult. No matter what it looked like his brain was beginning to acknowledge that he couldn't escape why he was here.

Pretty soon this lady with sympathetic eyes was going to ask him to confirm that Bella was dead. He wanted to say no. In his mind there was still room for a fantasy where this was all a big mix up. Maybe this was all just a typo, a period in the wrong spot, or a misspelled name. He knew that the authorities didn't make those kind of mistakes often. He just wanted to believe it so badly that he almost could.

He knew once they asked if it was Bella and he said yes, that it would be real. Bella would really be dead. He would really be as broken as the way Angel was looking at him now. Erroneous reached down and grabbed the seat of his chair to keep himself from leaving.

"We will try to make this as easy as possible." Angel was saying. "I am going to show you two pieces of paper. The first will be a picture of Bella." She continued.

"Ok." The two syllables barely crept out of his throat.

"The second paper will be a list of items found with Bella." Angel explained next. "Her belongings will be released to you when the case has been closed, but the detectives would like you to note anything that may be missing. It will help with the investigation."

This time Erroneous just nodded. Angel slid the first piece of paper face down across the table. He could feel his pulse begin to race. His breath became more shallow and quicker. Erroneous felt his fingers ache as his grip tightened on the seat beneath him.

"This is a picture of her face. She may not look quite the same as you remember." She said. "She may look"

"Dead." Erroneous said before he could stop himself.

"Right. Uh hrm yes… Take your time." She replied. "All you need to say is yes or no."

He slowly brought his hands onto the table and reached out for the paper. His fingers trembled as he flipped the picture over. The image was just a blur at first. It was like his eyes simply refused to see the worst fear of his life captured in still frame. After a moment they focused and his heart almost stopped.

In a way Angel was right. When Erroneous looked at the woman in the picture he didn't see Bella there at all. When he looked at Bella the whole world got quieter, colors became brighter, and it was easier to breath. The pale face in the photo looked just like Bella, but Erroneous didn't see her there at all.

"Is that your wife Mr. Truth?" Angel asked.

"No." He Thought.

"Yes." He answered quietly.

"Thank you." Angel said almost as quietly, gently removing the paper from his sight.

She slid another paper in front of him. This one was face up and appeared to be some sort of official form. Bella's name was at the top. As he scrolled down he saw that after a few lines of information and numbers there was a list labeled "victims belongings".

Each item on the list was specifically described. Bic Elite Ballpoint Pen Black, Cigarette Pack Marlboro Gold 100s count 13, Bic Lighter Yellow, Pair Skechers Slip Resistant Mary Jane Work Shoe. The list went on with the rest of her clothes, a handful of hair accessories and the remainder of what one might find in a pocket.

"The detectives said that your wife's purse was taken. Can you think of anything that may have been in it of value?" Angel prompted.

"No man knows what's in a woman's purse." Erroneous thought to himself.

"Her wallet and make up I guess." He answered. "I don't know what else."

"Okay." Angel continued. "Is there anything else that may have been taken? Did your wife wear any jewelry or carry any other valuables?"

"Bella only wore her wedding ring to work." Erroneous replied.

He looked back down at the list reading through it several more times. The ring wasn't there. He read through the list again more slowly, mouthing each item. He was blindsided by the sudden rush of emotion. Bile rose in the back of his throat and he swallowed it back down.

"Her ring isn't on the list." His voice sounded too loud in his head but quiet in the small room. "Is it still with her?" He asked, looking pleadingly at Angel.

"The list contains everything with her when she was brought here." Her eyes seemed to flinch as she said it. Erroneous imagined it was because she had seen him break some more. "I will let the detectives know." She said.

The police, since 1995, have only made an arrest in 16% of property crimes, 42% of violent crimes, and 62% of homicides. Bella's wedding ring was special. She designed it herself and Erroneous had it custom made. It had probably been the most expensive thing they owned, but it meant more than that.

The ring was white gold and looked kind of like a butterfly holding a perfect sapphire. Erroneous had argued for a diamond but Bella had insisted on a sapphire. Erroneous had bought the brightest most expensive one he could. He could not remember a day he felt more victorious than the day he put it on her finger.

"This ring is us." Bella had told him. "I'm the butterfly and you are the rare gem I have found."

Erroneous needed to find that ring. He needed that much of her back. Angel was still talking to him in that too kind voice, but Erroneous couldn't hear her. He said nothing as he stood up and walked out. By the time Angel had composed herself enough to catch up he was walking out the door of the building. He heard her call for him once, but didn't stop.

Chapter 6

"The only cure for grief is action."

-G.H. Lewes

Erroneous had once read that most burglars live within two miles of their targets. He didn't know if the same was true for armed robbers, but it was all he really had to go on. The image of Bella's blood drained face seemed superimposed over everything Erroneous looked at. He could feel her warm breath against his neck and hear her whispered "I love you" ringing in his ears.

"Was that today? Was that me?" He thought to himself.

The way he felt now contrasted so sharply with his memories from only a few hours ago. He could feel his hold on sanity slip at the sudden twist in reality. He had spent the last hour driving a grid around the area of the diner Bella worked at. He had driven every street, alley and cul-de-sac that didn't go directly by the scene of the crime. He just didn't know if he could take the sight of the last place he had seen her alive.

At first Erroneous had slowed down to look at every person he passed during his drive. This had turned up nothing but confused and suspicious return glares. He had no idea what to look for. Nobody he passed was wearing Bella's purse or a sign saying they had killed her. He could feel the realization of futility feed the fire of grief and desperation burning in his stomach.

Everything had been a haze since leaving the examiner's office. The internal dialogue that Erroneous used to keep himself present and centered was like an old antenna radio station. There were only small moments of clarity between the sounds of buzzing snow. The static was making it harder and harder to focus.

Erroneous used his prompts as handholds to help pull himself through his life. Now it was like the friction and gravity of his mind had ceased. Nearly everything slipped through his mental grasp. What he did catch seemed to send him spinning away as if Erroneous himself had no substance or weight.

A little red light shaped like a gas pump lit up on his dash. U.S. fuel economy hit 24.7 mpg in 2016. Erroneous grasped on desperately to the thought. There was a gas station on the next corner and he turned in pulling up to an empty pump. He rolled down his window and opened his wallet for his debit card.

Once again he was met with the past image of them all laughing. It was a stark reminder of what he had lost. Bella's smiling, shining face gazed at him as if mocking the pale reflection he had been forced to endure earlier. The attendant approached the window and Erroneous distractedly handed over the debit card.

"Fill it up." Erroneous mumbled.

"$20 regular?" The attendant replied.

Erroneous simply nodded yes, his eyes still glued to the photo in his wallet. He and Bella had been together for a while by then. He had asked Bella to marry him shortly after it had been taken. He had been out of jail for just over a year. She had waited for him while he was in.

He was amazed that she had. He couldn't remember ever being happier. He thought he was finally getting his due after all the unfair crap life had buried him in. To Erroneous it felt like his life had finally left bumpy dirt roads behind and hit smooth asphalt for the first time.

Erroneous and Dante had moved to Portland for a fresh start. Their fortunes in California had taken a turn for the worse and Dante saw the "Weird" northwest city as a prime landing spot for a couple of counter culture entrepreneurs like themselves. Dante liked to call them that, "Counter Culture Entrepreneurs". Erroneous liked Dante's alternative labels. They helped him look at things from a different angle and feel better about them.

"Most of the time, what something is, isn't as important as how you look at it." Dante liked to tell him.

They moved into a small house with a garage in the cheapest neighborhood they could find. It had only cost them $600 a month and utilities were included. Back then Portland was an affordable place to live. You could pay your rent and still feed yourself.

Three months after moving in they were harvesting their first crop. By then Erroneous had become very good at growing marijuana. Dante called it science turned into art. Erroneous enjoyed all the intricacies and quite frankly liked being around his plants more than people.

Portland is the strip club capital of the U.S. and Dante had

tried working them first, for obvious reasons. As it turned out that

strippers preferred meth to weed and were used to having things just

given to them. Most of the customer's money went to the strippers of

course. Much to Dante's disappointment the strip clubs weren't ideal

but once they discovered the dive bars in the bohemian Hawthorne

District their fortunes changed.

The neighborhood was infested with Trustafarians with

plenty of money and nothing to do but smoke weed and talk about

saving the world. Portland had always been known for good weed.

Prices were lower than California and it was too far north to be

inundated with Mexican schwag. Erroneous' buds still hit the street

like a sledgehammer. Nobody had smoked anything like it.

Everybody loved their flower. On a good weekend they could

sell a pound while bar hopping on Hawthorne and Belmont. Fifty-

two percent of people have tried pot over the course of their lifetime

and forty-four percent of those that have continue to use it

throughout their lives. Finding someone in the Hawthorne District

that didn't smoke pot was like getting struck by lightning. Dante did

all of the selling but he insisted on bringing Erroneous with him.

"You can't spend your whole life locked in a room talking to plants." Dante used to tell him.

At the time Erroneous would have loved to do just that. Dante was good with people and always seemed comfortable in social situations even with strangers. Erroneous wasn't. He spent most of his time nursing a beer and quietly observing from a corner booth.

He was sitting in one of those corner booths on a Sunday night the first time he heard Bella sing. It was Gold Dust Woman and he had never heard Stevie Nicks sing it half as well. Maybe it was the beer or the stage lights and haziness of the smoky bar, but when Erroneous first set eyes on Bella it felt like a dream.

Erroneous started to practice singing the next day and Dante didn't have to drag him out to the bars anymore. Erroneous made sure they came to the same place every Sunday. The first couple times Bella wasn't there and he found himself wondering if it had been a dream. The third time she was there and the saying "third time's a charm" became a personal mantra of his for a long while afterwards.

It was another month before he actually spoke to her. He had finally worked up the courage to sing the song he had been practicing. A Gallup poll once found that forty percent of American adults have a fear of public speaking or "stage fright". The encouragement she gave him in the face of his withering resolve did more than she would ever know. For the first time ever, Erroneous Conception Truth, felt confident. He had felt smart and brave and even competent or knowledgeable before, but nothing like this. Something about the way she looked at him made him, for the first time, really believe in himself.

Cheap Trick would have been proud of the enthusiasm, if not the talent, of his performance of I Want You To Want Me. He had picked it because everyone liked it and it didn't seem to require a beautiful singing voice to pull off. He only had to belt out the first line while looking at Bella's smiling face to discover he meant every word he was singing.

Everyone cheered and clapped when he was done. "I love that song!" Bella shouted at him.

He gave her an awkward bow and then almost ran from the stage as he once again began to feel the pressure of everyone's attention. Erroneous had never done anything even remotely like this before. He focused on calming his breathing, but couldn't help sneaking a fleeting look at Bella's table when he passed. She was still watching him too and he felt the heat in his cheeks intensify. Dante was waiting at his booth with a fresh beer and a Cheshire cat grin.

"She must be magic." Dante laughed at him. "I never thought in all my days I would see you singing with your eyes closed in front of a group of strangers."

"Who?" Erroneous asked trying to deflect.

"Don't try and bullshit me E." Dante countered. "You may be the brains here, but I'm not a fool. One day it's pulling teeth to get you out of that grow room. The next thing I know you are dragging me here every Sunday like its church."

Dante was waving over the server. "You should buy her a drink." He said.

"Who?" Erroneous tried again.

Dante laughed harder. "We have come here every week for two months and there is only one person I have seen you look at for more than five seconds." Dante answered. "That is who."

Erroneous didn't respond but ordered a Hefeweizen with an orange slice when the server got to their table. It was what Bella always seemed to be drinking. Dante had to let the server know it was for Bella and added another beer for each of the girls in her group to the order. Erroneous stared nervously into his own beer, wondering how the drink would be received, as the server walked away.

It was getting late in the night, Erroneous was sitting at the booth alone while Dante played a game of pool, when Bella stood up from her group of friends and began walking towards the bar. He was sure that she was simply going for another drink until she changed course and walked right up to him expectantly. This was as close as he had ever been to her. He couldn't bring himself to look up. Just the smell of her made his heart beat so hard he thought he might pass out.

"So what's up?" She said. "Buy a girl a drink, but don't come over to say hi or even look at her the rest of the night?"

Her voice was teasing but Erroneous still felt himself panic at the thought that he might have truly offended her. His voice felt stuck in his stomach and his eyes seemed glued to the glass of pilsner in front of him. He was having trouble believing that she was actually talking to him. Part of him felt like he would break the spell and the moment would disappear if he so much as moved.

"What's the matter, not pretty enough for ya?" She asked.

"You're very pretty." He finally spoke, a little shaken by her continued attention.

"Really?" She teased.

"Really." He confirmed. "You're pretty like the sunrise."

"I guess sunrises are nice enough." She said sounding a bit unimpressed.

"They are more than just nice. Every time I see the sunrise it is a little bit different, but just as amazing." Erroneous continued. "When I see it I know that no matter what was before, it is a new day with new hope. You are pretty like that." He looked up at her intently for just a moment then back down at his beer.

When he asked her years later why she had ever given him a chance she said, "I have probably had a million men look at me in my life, but you were the only one that made me feel seen."

They got married on December 21st, 2012. Bella had picked the date. He had once told her that the end of the world couldn't keep him from being with her. Everyone brought survival themed wedding gifts. Bella had thought herself so clever until they ended up with a year's supply of toilet paper to go along with their new fishing gear.

They probably would have been married earlier if it wasn't for what Bella called "that night". They had met some of Bella's friends at a dive bar in the Lents neighborhood for karaoke. The song selection had been terrible but the drinks were cheap. Erroneous had a good buzz, but Bella was falling down drunk when they left.

They walked to the Holgate MAX station even though the Foster station was closer. It wasn't so much a decision as a stumble in the wrong direction for too long. Erroneous remembered being relieved when they arrived. Bella had already fallen down twice and he was looking forward to them both being safe and sitting for a little while.

They were heading down the stairs to the platform. Erroneous hadn't even noticed the person coming up the stairs until Bella was stumbling into them. He caught Bella before she fell, but the impact had been enough to push the other person off balance.

Erroneous reached out with one hand but barely brushed the fabric

of their coat before they tumbled backwards down the stairs all the

way to the platform. They never moved again.

Dante had always told him. "Cops get paid, so keep your

mouth shut and let them do their own work."

Erroneous repeated this to Bella as they waited for the

ambulance and police to show up. As soon as they did arrive,

Erroneous took blame for the entire thing before they could even ask

Bella a question. Bella received a charge of public intoxication and

had to spend a night sobering up and pay a fine. The next day she

didn't even remember what had happened.

Erroneous however was arrested, charged and convicted of

second degree manslaughter. People with felony convictions account

for 8% of the U.S. population. On camera, his attempt to catch the

person looked very much like a push and the prosecution insisted

that it was. He tried to tell them it wasn't, but it didn't even seem

like his own public defender believed him. Even though his prior

conviction had been as a juvenile, the judge said it showed a history

of reckless decisions.

By the end of his trial Erroneous was completely in shock. He couldn't believe what was happening. He was sentenced to a year in prison and 10 years parole. The extended parole was due to "a perceived lack of remorse" by the board. Erroneous couldn't have felt worse about what had happened, he just didn't know how to show them.

The next year had been the worst of his life. He never talked to anyone about it, not even Dante. He requested solitary confinement right away, but was sent to the infirmary twice before it was granted. He had spent most of his time reading. Partly for the constant flow of information, mostly because he had learned that having a thick book in your grasp can come in handy. Bella wrote him every week and was there when he was released. Seeing her then made it all worth it in Erroneous' mind.

Chapter 7

"If I cease searching, then, woe is me, I am lost. That is how I look

at it - keep going, keep going come what may."

— Vincent van Gogh

Erroneous was startled from his thoughts by a knock on the window. "Your card was declined." The gas station attendant informed him. "Do you have a different one?"

"What?" Erroneous asked. "It should work."

"Ran it three times." The attendant responded.

"Ok." He took the card back. "Thank you anyway."

Erroneous pulled out of the gas station and parked on the street a block down. More than half of Americans have less than one thousand dollars in their bank account. He was positive that there was money in his account. He had just been paid a couple days ago.

Erroneous dug his phone out of his pocket, there were several missed calls from Dante. He didn't know what to say yet so he had just put the ringer on silent. He opened up his bank app and saw that there had been a withdrawal of the maximum amount. It was at a bank on the corner of Hawthorne and Caesar Chavez Blvd. A couple other large purchases at stores in that same area had put the account in overdraft.

It took him a moment before he remembered that they had taken Bella's purse. Erroneous screamed and pounded the steering wheel. They just wouldn't stop taking from him. The anger burned some of the haze away and gave him a small amount of clarity.

It had been just a little more than an hour since the last time the card had been used at a smoke shop. There could be a chance that Bella's killers were still in that area. It was the dimmest of lights on such a dark day but better than the complete darkness of just a moment earlier. He looked up the address of the last purchase.

"I know where that is." Erroneous whispered. "I will get your ring back. I promise."

He estimated that he still had enough gas to make it there. After that he would walk the whole city if he had to. He started the car and headed toward the Hawthorne District. That area of

Hawthorne was always crowded, which he wasn't looking forward

to. He parked a couple blocks north and walked towards the corner

of Caesar Chavez and Hawthorne. All of the transactions on the card

took place within a few blocks of that spot so he figured he could

start there and work his way down the street.

As Erroneous approached the corner he could see there was

already a cop standing in front of The Hawthorne Theatre. The

officer was standing directly across the street from the bank where

Bella's card had been used. The Portland Police Bureau has

approximately 1,000 full-time officers.

The officer was stopping passersby and showing them a

photo. Erroneous' instincts told him to avoid the police, but he knew

there could be a chance that the cop was looking for the same people

he was. He took a few seconds to weight the risk. Deciding that any

risk was worth it he started across the street.

As he stepped out of the crosswalk Erroneous headed

towards the officer. He tried to blend in with the flow of foot traffic

passing the cop on the sidewalk, but there were too many people

walking by and they were too close. Erroneous didn't like being around too many people at the same time. It was like he could feel everyone's looks and thoughts and feelings and he had to pay attention to them all.

It was a sensation like the tingling and stinging of strong winds blowing sand against his skin. He could feel himself become instantly more tense and agitated as his eyes and ears and nose tried to hear and see and smell everything and everyone. The input was overwhelming for a moment and he had to stop. He rubbed his temples with the tips of his fingers for a few breaths as passing people lightly jostled him.

"Sir, are you okay?" A voice broke through the building headache. "Sir?"

Erroneous looked up to find the officer standing in front of him with a concerned look. "Uh, I'm fine." Erroneous replied. "Just a headache." At least 1 in 7 adults are affected by migraine headaches

"The worst." The officer said. "I was hoping you could help." He continued holding up a picture. "We are looking for this girl. Have you seen her?"

The girl in the picture had a very natural smile, the kind that always looked sincere in photographs. She was wearing a light blue dress with a small white flower print. Her face and hair were clean and she looked more alive in the picture, but Erroneous still recognized her as the homeless girl he had seen while dropping Bella off at work. She had to be involved or at least seen something. It was too much of a coincidence.

"Do you recognize her?" the officer asked.

Erroneous realized that he had been staring at the picture. "No." He answered.

"Are you sure?" The officer pressed.

"I'm not actually. I may have seen her out in southeast close to 122nd." Erroneous could tell that the officer was suspicious and hoped his answer would satisfy him.

It wasn't a lie, the diner Bella worked at was on 122nd. The diner Bella used to work at Erroneous corrected in his head. He felt the pain of the correction like a deep stab in his chest and behind his eyes. It made his ears ring.

"When?" The officer seemed eager at the positive sighting.

"I don't remember." Erroneous lied hoping the officer would let it go.

The cop reached into his front shirt pocket and pulled out a card. "If you see her again, or remember anything else please give me a call." He held the card out to Erroneous.

"I will do that." Erroneous took it and put it in his back pocket.

"Thanks." The officer looked at him again a little curiously before Erroneous awkwardly walked past him and continued down the street leaving the cop to stare at his back as he walked away.

Erroneous swore he could feel the officer's eyes, but when he stopped a block away and looked back the blue uniform was nowhere to be seen. He took a minute to compose himself and steady his breath again. He was looking through a store window. Inside a man was holding up to pair of socks. One was green and the other was blue, but other than that they appeared to be identical. The man studied them intensely as if looking for a difference.

As many as eight percent of men and 0.5 percent of women are colorblind. Socks are one of the items most needed by homeless shelters. Over sixty-six percent of homeless people say addiction was a major cause of their homelessness. The easiest place to get

hard drugs was downtown. Erroneous could remember several times

someone had offered him or Dante some black tar or crystal meth

while they were downtown at night. If the girl had been the one to

use Bella's card, then he was sure her next stop would be downtown

to pick up a fix.

He headed that direction at a purposeful pace. Erroneous

tried to stay focused, but it was difficult in such a busy environment

and especially with everything that had happened. He didn't want to

miss seeing the girl, but it was becoming overwhelming trying to

look everywhere at once. It quickly became too much. He let himself

sink deep into his inner dialogue, hoping his natural awareness

wouldn't let him down.

Hawthorne Blvd was originally named "U" Street then

became Asylum Avenue in 1883. Then in 1888 they changed the

name to Hawthorne Avenue in honor of Dr. J.C. Hawthorne, who

co-founded Oregon's first mental hospital. It became Hawthorne

Blvd in 1933. The Bagdad Theater opened in 1927 and was listed on

the National Register of Historic Places in 1989.

Portland's public transportation system began in 1872 and consisted of horse and mule drawn carts. Before the great depression Portland had an electric rail car system that stretched over 27 miles all the way to Estacada. After the Great depression the extensive electric rail system was replaced by a more consolidated bus system. The electric rail system would return to Portland in the form of the Metropolitan Area Express, or MAX, in 1986. Portland now has 84.3 miles of light rail and 688 buses operating on 85 routes.

The median age of a Portland resident is 36.7 years old. Over 17% of Portland's population is between the ages of 25 and 34. The average cost of living for a single person in the Portland area is estimated to be approximately $965 without rent. With average studio rent being $901 the combined monthly cost estimate for a single person is about $1866. That is $22,392 a year. According to the 2016 census the annual real median personal income in the U.S. was $31,099. That falls into a federal tax bracket of fifteen percent and a state tax bracket of nine percent. After taxes $31,099 becomes approximately $23,630. This leaves $103.18 left over for the average single person in Portland every month after expenses.

Financial advisors say you should have twice your yearly salary saved by age thirty-five. If you began working at eighteen and over the course of your working career you averaged the current personal median income of $31,099, stayed single, and you saved every extra cent, you would be over 68 years old before you reached that recommended savings goal. Erroneous almost didn't see her. She wasn't on Hawthorne, but by luck he happened to spot her crossing the street at the same time as he was, but a block up on Madison. He recognized the too large jacket even from a distance.

He rushed to the next corner and waited. After a few long moments she showed up at the corner a block away and crossed the street. He had left the busy part of Hawthorne a few blocks earlier, so it should be easier to keep track of her without all of the people. She had to be heading downtown.

Erroneous wanted to talk to her before she got there and he lost her in the downtown business. Madison and Hawthorne met at the Hawthorne Bridge and you had to cross the bridge to get downtown. He decided to keep paralleling her course until then. Once they were on the bridge there wouldn't be anywhere for her to run and he might be able to confront her.

Erroneous followed her like this for 1,213 steps, but when he got to the corner of 11th avenue and looked a block up she wasn't there. He waited for the lights to change twice, but there was no sign of her. He ran back to the corner of 12th and looked but she wasn't there either, so he walked up to Madison and walked from 12th back down to 11th. He didn't see her anywhere in either direction.

He wondered if he had missed her somehow but that didn't make sense. She wasn't running and even if she was she wouldn't have been so fast that he couldn't see her somewhere down the street. Maybe she had noticed him following her or maybe something else had spooked her. She had probably found a place to hide, but Erroneous had no idea where. He couldn't exactly just go around poking in bushes and digging through dumpsters yelling "come out, come out wherever you are" like a twisted game of hide and seek.

He was still positive she was heading downtown. The Hawthorne Bridge was the closest most direct route. He decided to find a spot to watch the bridge and hope he was right. The Hawthorne Bridge opened in 1910, is 1,382 feet in length, and was added to the Register of Historic Places in 2012.

On the east side there are several ways for foot traffic to get onto the bridge. You could follow Hawthorne directly onto the bridge where it starts. You can also continue down Madison and walk up the stairs next to the bus stop on the corner of Water, or you can keep going down Madison and take the path up from the East Bank Esplanade. This will put you on the bridge right before it starts over the Willamette River.

If Erroneous just stood on the bridge and waited she would spot him from a mile away. He decided to set up watch by the East Bank Esplanade path. That would give him the best chance of seeing her no matter which side of the bridge she crossed and would hopefully keep her from seeing him until she was already on the main span. Then she wouldn't have any place to run or hide and he might be able to get some answers.

He made his way down to the esplanade and found a spot behind a concrete pillar that gave him a view of the bridge walkway, but kept him hidden from anybody walking up until they were already past. He leaned his back up against the pillar, let out a long breath and settled in to hope and wait. He had no idea what he was doing or how he had gotten here. There were so many things that could have changed today. A failed morning alarm or a traffic jam and Bella might have shown up too late to be killed. Things like that happen all of the time. Why couldn't have one of them happened to him and Bella this morning.

She was gone now and Erroneous was completely lost. He had never really had any big goals or ambitions. As long as he had food and clothes, housing that wasn't prison and nobody was attacking him, Erroneous was content. He had only ever had one plan. That was to be with Bella forever. Someone had taken that now. They had taken her and with her, everything.

He thought about that first night again. Until that night Erroneous had never really talked to the opposite sex outside of the social necessities of greetings and polite small talk. He wasn't comfortable starting conversations with anybody much less the mysterious and powerful fairer sex. There also weren't a lot of women standing in line to talk to the weird quiet guy sitting alone in a corner.

The few opportunities that did come up had ended awkwardly. Whenever he found himself in that situation it felt like his body and mind shot into overload. He became terrified of what he would say or do so ended up just sitting there like lump. It had never taken long for them to walk away leaving Erroneous feeling embarrassed and impotent.

It hadn't been like that with Bella. He was still just as terrified, but Bella was different. It was like she didn't have the same expectation as the other women that had approached him. She seemed genuinely interested in who he was and not just disappointed in who he wasn't. After their initial exchange that night she had sat down next to him in the booth.

"You should buy me another drink." she said matter-of-factly.

"Ok." The server wasn't around so Erroneous got up and went to the bar. He ordered another beer for them both. When he returned with their drinks he couldn't help but be a little stunned that Bella was still sitting there. She was staring at him like he was a puzzle.

"I don't think I have ever heard you sing before." Bella said as he walked up.

"It was my first time. I hope I didn't ruin it." Erroneous confirmed self-consciously.

Bella let out a small laugh. "Karaoke is like dancing. You don't have to be good at it. You just do it. It just helps you feel, ya know."

Erroneous just nodded at her statement. He did know. He wasn't sure if it was the karaoke, but he did feel more than he maybe ever had before. The rush left him light headed.

"You don't talk much." She said. "Very mysterious." She gave him slightly devious look and he felt more blood rise to his face.

"I'm uh, I'm not really that comfortable around people." Erroneous kind of mumbled as he set her beer down and settled himself into his seat.

"Well people are usually a greedy, selfish, destructive bunch of assholes so that is probably a mark in your favor." She laughed a little as she said it. "Do I make you uncomfortable?" She asked.

"Yes." Erroneous answered almost too quickly. He watched her mouth drop to a slight frown. "But not in a bad way like everybody else." He continued

"You make me feel uncomfortable in the most amazing way, like I know something great is about to happen." He explained.

She tilted her head to the side and seemed to examine him for a second before a slight smile raised her lips. "My name is Bella." She said holding out her hand.

He felt so inadequate sitting there next to someone so beautiful and nice. He took her hand like it would break. He didn't know if he should kiss it like a queen or shake it like a business meeting. He felt way out of his element. After a second he settled for an awkward kind of jiggle before letting go.

"I'm Erroneous, um Erroneous Truth." He hated saying it out loud. It felt like saying I'm a mistake and nobody wants me.

"Really?" She said with curiosity instead of the usual mocking tone he had come to expect.

"Yeah. I know it's stupid." Erroneous felt mortified. "Dante just calls me E."

There was an awkward moment of silence. Bella looked thoughtful. Erroneous was sure that she was thinking about how to get away from him. It was the reaction he had come to expect.

"You know." She finally spoke. "Our names are the first lies we tell somebody. We say I am so and so, but we aren't. We are so much more than some tag assigned by someone who was meeting us for the first time. In my opinion all names are lies, at least your name has the decency to say so." She continued. "That probably makes your name my favorite so far."

Erroneous was stunned. Nobody had ever treated him like this before. In that moment the whole world changed for Erroneous. A door had opened in his mind and when he looked through it he saw something he had never seen before.

For the first time he saw a life where it was ok to be Erroneous Conception Truth. He saw a world where he could be accepted and maybe even loved. Bella could never understand the importance of what she had given him in that moment. Erroneous wasn't even sure he truly understood the significance that moment had in his life.

"Erroneous is a little awkward to say though." Bella said interrupting his thoughts. "And E is a little too gangsta for my taste. I think I am going to call you Ron if that's okay." She finished.

"I'd like that." Erroneous responded, thinking that she could call him anything she wanted if it meant she would keep talking to him.

They had sat in that corner booth talking until closing time. He had never felt anything like what he felt that night. Now that Bella was gone he didn't think he would ever feel that way again. He could almost feel the door that opened in his mind that night slamming shut again.

Chapter 8

"Drugs are a bet with your mind."

— Jim Morrison

Tanda watched the creepy janitor looking guy from a slit

between the boards in the abandoned furniture store. She hadn't been

sure that he was even following her, but on a day like today it was

better not to take any chances. She had noticed him looking at her a

few blocks ago. Once you spent enough time on the streets

everybody in a uniform began to stand out like a sore thumb. Not

just cops but all of the maintenance, and janitor, and security that

end up hassling you and running you off. Everyone in a uniform

became suspect.

She had been looking for a spot to hideout and was lucky

when she found a gap at the top of a broken out, boarded up window just big enough for her to squeeze through. Especially lucky since her belly seemed to be getting bigger every day. The building was basically empty except for some scrap boards and probably rodents. The only light came from cracks in the boarded up windows. Dust floated lazily in the beams.

She figured she would hang tight for an hour or so then continue downtown to meet up with Jip and Cam's stupid asses. What a fucking pain. First Pig Dad shows up and she has to hide until he dipped out and now this fucking guy. Jip and Cam were going to be pissed that she was taking so long, but fuck them. What was she supposed to do?

Today wasn't supposed to go like this. It was supposed to be simple and easy not a total fucking disaster. They should already be on their way to some beach town to live happily ever after. Instead they were running around town like a bunch of fucking rats trying not to get caught. Yay for Jip and all his great fucking ideas.

She put her hand under her shirt and rubbed the ever growing bulge of her belly. It was strange to have something alive and growing inside. Most of the time she tried not to think about it.

Sometimes she could feel it move. It was easier to ignore before that.

Now every nudge from inside tilted her world more.

She didn't know if it was Jip's or not. Things can get pretty

hazy when you party with Beyonce. She and Jip were going to

pretend like it was his at least. They were going to use the money

from today to run away from this fucking city. They would find a

little place next to the ocean, get clean and raise their kid right, not

like everyone else in this fucked up society.

Jip always told her that they weren't homeless, they were

free. His mom left when he was real young and his dad had died

when he was sixteen. Instead of going into the foster system, Jip had

run away to the street. He liked to say his Dad was his hero for all

the wrong reasons.

His dad had taught him that you could work hard every day.

You could work late every night. You could work weekends. You

can do everything they want you to do. Still someday you could be

on your way home from work, late at night, after working a double

on a weekend, get pushed down some stairs and it doesn't matter. It

was all for nothing.

Jip was always going on about how he wasn't going to be a slave to the system and how his old man had died a martyr. He was a big fan of the occupy movement. At first it had been super exciting and romantic. She had met Jip on the street after running away from home. He was older and seemed like he knew so much.

He told her that she had been right to run away. That the only way to change the world was to not be a part of a broken system. Jip showed her how to survive on the street. He gave her drugs and protected her. He had made her feel good when she needed to. It was a grand adventure. Way better than her life before, at least at first.

Things changed after a while. Everything became about the drugs. Jip was impossible to be around when they were dry. He would hit her sometimes. When things got real bad he would find someone for her to sleep with and they would use the money for drugs. It had only happened a few times. The first time was the worst. It was easier the next couple. She knew that she deserved it.

Tanda had never told Jip that she wasn't running away because the system was broken. She didn't want him to know the shitty person she really was. Tanda had ran away because she was broken and she broke everything she cared about. She was trying to throw herself away so she didn't hurt anyone anymore. If she was as brave as her sister had been then she would have killed herself too.

Tanda could remember when she found out she was getting a baby sister. She had wanted one so bad. Her little sister would be her best friend. They would play dolls and do each other's hair. It would be amazing.

"Your Daddy and I decided to have another little girl so that you can have a baby sister and friend." Her mother had told her.

"I am going to be the best big sister ever!" Tanda had remembered bragging.

Nobody told her that she was going to have to give up her mother to have a sister. Tanda took it out on her sister, but she knew her mother's death was her own fault. If she hadn't wanted a little sister so bad than her mother would still be alive. If things had been enough for her the way they were, or if she had been enough for her parents, they wouldn't have needed to have another child and Tanda would be home with her mother right now.

A year ago her sister had come to her and told her about the kids at school picking on her. She told Tanda about the notes in her locker and the posts online from other students. They called her ugly and stupid and worthless. Some boy she liked had put her online info in all the bathrooms and spread a rumor that she had sex with him and a bunch of his friends. Her Facebook was full of people calling her a whore and several girls at school had tried to beat her up.

"I just feel like killing myself." She remembered her sister telling her.

"Maybe you should." Tanda had said cold and heartlessly like only a bitter teenager can.

Her sister had been thirteen. Her dad had sent Tanda to get her for breakfast the next morning. That's when Tanda found her hanging from the closet bar. Her sister's face was almost black as she hung there in her nightgown. As soon as she saw her she knew it was her fault. She knew her selfishness had killed her sister just like it had killed her mother.

She stayed for a few months because she thought her dad needed her, but once he brought home "Miss Susie Sympathy", she bailed. He had someone to take care of him now and Angel was a way better person than she was, even if she was a saccharin bitch. Plenty of people had told her that it wasn't her fault. They told her, when her mother died, that it wasn't her fault. They told her, when her sister died, that it wasn't her fault. It was just something people said. It was something they said when they didn't know.

She was starting to feel sick. Her stomach churned and her mouth filled with saliva. She didn't know if it was the baby, the fucked up day, or if she just needed a hit soon. It was probably all three.

They had gotten enough cash from the diner to rent a motel room on 82nd. From there, they had gone to the bank to get more cash. Stupid bitch had her pin number in her wallet. Jip was going to buy as much shit as he could get with it and they were going to sell it. It would take longer, but Jip promised it would be enough for them to leave still. She had used the rest of the money on the card to buy cigarettes and gift cards. She was supposed to text them and meet up with them downtown. Then they would head to the motel from there.

She was tempted to just go back to the room alone and wait, but there was no telling how long those losers would take, and she wasn't going to get off until they were back. If she met up with them she could probably get a little bump to keep the edge off. Fuck knows she needed some. Just one more good launch to get over this fucked up day and into a new life. Then she would stop, for the baby.

She pulled out her phone to text Jip and let him know she was going to take longer, but it was dead. She fished the charging cable out of one of the deep pockets in her coat and began looking for an outlet. Once she found one she plugged it in and sat down to chill. She really wished she had some fucking "H", or pot, or fucking anything right now. Just something to keep the itch away until later. She lit a cigarette instead.

Tanda remembered her first time riding the white horse. Jip had told her it would take away her pain, open her mind, and make her feel free. He was right. It just made everything go away. It made the whole world warm and fuzzy.

People think that the euphoria is why you can't stop. Tanda knew it was more than that. It made your pain go away for a little while, and that was the true addiction. Then the real world would come back and it was even shittier than you remember so you have to do it all over again, and again, and again.

It was better than love. It was stronger than love. It could kill your love. That was the real magic. Loving people, loving yourself, is what causes all of the pain. Nothing killed love like a good "H Bomb".

Tanda wished she could be blasted away now. Cold sweat damped her face as she sat in the dusty dimly lit building. She could see the lady's face from this morning. It would change into the face of her sister and then her mother, then back again. Tanda put her face in her hands and cried.

She woke up a little while later feeling even more sick to her stomach. She started to crawl to a corner, but thought, what is the point? It isn't like she lived here. She puked right where she was.

Fuck, she was feeling shaky. She unplugged her phone and checked for messages. There were none. Assholes didn't even care that they hadn't heard from her yet. They were probably already high. She was jealous and pissed.

She sent Jip a text. "I'm fine, in case you were wondering." She continued tapping the keys. "Will be at Hawthorne Bridge in twenty. Better be there and better have something, fucktard."

She peaked out between the boards to make sure there was nobody on the street watching. The clouds had come in to cover the sun and it was drizzling. Standard Portland weather. Liquid sunshine some called it.

"It is always pissing on us." Tanda whispered to herself.

It was also starting to get dark outside. Tanda was grateful for that. Being a homeless drug addict during the daytime was like being a roach caught out when the lights turn on. She always felt way more comfortable after the sun had set.

She gathered up some boards and placed them under the window she had come in through. Everything was way harder now that her withdrawals were making her feel like shit. Eventually she managed to use the boards as a makeshift stool and pull herself onto the window sill and back through the space at the top. She tried to lower herself down gently, but ended up falling the last few feet to land hard on her ass.

"Fuck!" She half yelled.

Everything hurt more when you were on the bad end of a come down. It was like getting back all the feelings you buried at the same time. She hoped Jip and Cam had hooked up. She really needed to get some wings before she hit the ground hard, again.

She felt her phone vibrate and pulled it back out of her pocket. It was a message from Jip. "All good. We'll be there. Don't be a bitch." It read.

"Fuck you Jip." She said to the screen as she gathered herself up off of the ground.

She pulled her baggy coat tighter around herself and started in the direction of downtown. As long as Jip and Cam didn't flake they could catch the MAX and be at the motel in a little less than an hour. If they sold everything fast, they could be out of town by the weekend. First she just needed a little to keep everything stable, but not too much because the baby.

She had just reached the main span of the bridge crossing the river when she heard something and glanced back. A little ways back was the fucking janitor walking towards her. Seeing him jolted her slightly from her withdrawal fog. She knew for sure now that he was following her. Her blood pumped like hammers in her veins as she turned and ran.

Chapter 9

"People that get their feet wet must learn to take their medicine."

-P.L. Travers

The only thing that had kept Erroneous waiting around was

that he had no idea what else to do. After the first hour, the clouds

had thickened and it had begun to precipitate. It wasn't standard rain,

but more of just a thick wet mist. The rain didn't feel like it was

falling on you, so much as it felt like you were walking through it.

He was amazed at all of the different ways a place like Portland

could find to make you wet and cold.

He wished he had brought his jacket, but if he was being

honest, it seemed fitting. A large part of him wished it would rain

harder. He wanted the wind to howl and rip off roofs. He wanted the

water to pound and flood the streets. He wanted some part of the outside world to reflect the turmoil and emptiness he felt inside himself.

Erroneous lived all of his life with a certain level of disquietude. It was a fear that he accepted. Until Bella, life had never given him any reason to doubt the validity of his fears. She had always said she admired the way he wore his fear.

"I know what people see when they look at me. They see a weirdo that is always afraid." He had told her one day. "The truth is I am afraid, and I understand if that makes you see me a certain way. I just want you to know that I will do anything for you no matter how afraid I am. I need you to know that I love you more than anyone ever will."

He had been struggling to find work after getting out of prison. He couldn't keep growing pot while on parole and it was the only work experience he had. Erroneous wasn't much at interviews and didn't have a resume. Combine that with being a felon and he had been turned down by just about every available employer in the Portland metro.

He had been worried that Bella would see him as a failure. She deserved someone strong and successful. He knew everyone viewed him as weak. He knew everyone saw that he was unsure and afraid when they looked at him. He knew that his timid and reticent way just confirmed to most people that their observation was correct.

"Everybody is afraid." She told him. "You are just the only person I know that doesn't lie about it."

"It doesn't seem like everyone else is afraid." He replied.

"That's because, unlike you, they aren't strong enough or courageous enough to honestly face their life and their fear." Bella countered. "You walk through this life with a honesty and tenacity that most people could never come close to. You have the fortitude to walk in the open while they hide. You think they treat you different because they look at you and see you as weak and scared, but that isn't true. People react to you that way because they look at you and see how afraid and weak they are."

She had started to gain a certain amount of vehemence as she spoke. "When those kind of people look at you they feel shamed and exposed, and they should. They try and cover their fear with anger and hate. They attack you because they aren't strong enough to face themselves. Those are the kind of people I wish I could cut out of my life, Ron, not you. I love you and I believe in you."

Erroneous hadn't believed he could love her any more than he already did, but when she had finished speaking it felt like his heart was too big for his chest. That was the magic of Bella for him. In her eyes he became strong and amazing. She made the world a place Erroneous belonged. Or used to.

He wished she was here to make him feel like that now. He wished he could feel anything other than what he felt right now. He wished he could even just be afraid again. Even that would be better than his current torture.

Fear is what you feel when you think the worst could happen. It is what you feel when something bad could happen. What he felt now was something past fear. What Erroneous felt now was what you feel after what you feared has already happened.

With fear there was still a sense of purpose. There was something to do or not do. There was still time. There was hope that you could stop what you fear from happening. What he felt now was fear realized. It was devoid of hope. It was just agony and desolation.

His mind ran through all of the different ways he could have saved Bella and didn't. Why didn't he have a better job so she didn't have to work? Why didn't he know she was in danger? If he had

been smarter and better he could have changed everything. So many

whys and ifs. He should have taken better care of her. He had failed

to protect the only thing in his life he valued. Now all he could do

was try and keep his promise and get back her ring.

He realized that what he was doing was crazy. He should

have talked to the police and let them handle it. He shouldn't be out

here stalking some homeless girl that may or may not know anything

about his wife's murder. He just couldn't imagine going home and

sitting there alone. The pain dictated that he do something. He could

feel it filling his insides with fire and he knew if he stopped it would

devour him.

As the sky darkened into night, Erroneous resigned himself

to sitting by the bridge and waiting forever or until the rain froze him

to death. He was sure that he had missed her during the rush hour

traffic going over the bridge or she had changed direction and never

gone over the bridge at all. He had ran across the bridge twice, once

on each side. He did it just in case she had already passed, but was

still on the bridge. Both times he didn't see her and sprinted back to

his look out spot hoping that he hadn't missed her passing there. He was starting to become desperate and frantic. He could feel his panic

rising up and threatening to consume what little sanity he had left.

He was so far into his depression that, when she did pass, he

almost didn't move to follow. His mind almost didn't believe his

eyes and it took a moment for everything to register. He could

almost feel something trickle down his spine, giving him just enough

to get up and go after her. It wasn't hope as much as just a slight

releasing of resignation.

He kept his distance as he trailed her onto the main span of

the bridge. Getting somebody's attention was not one of Erroneous'

well developed skills. Even without the surrounding circumstances,

he was way out of his comfort zone. He had no idea what he was

going to say if he caught up to her.

"Did you kill my wife? Do you have her ring?" He knew that

would not work out the way he wanted.

He finally worked up the fortitude to call out. "Excuse me.

Ma'am? Excuse me."

The sound of his voice contrasted with everything in his

mind. It was timid and polite. He found himself irritated that it

lacked the frenzy he felt. He tried again.

"Hey!" He screamed at the top of his lungs.

The girl turned and looked at him. Everything seemed to freeze for a heartbeat. Their eyes met. Then she turned around and started running away from him across the bridge.

Erroneous broke into a sprint after her. He didn't know what to do if he caught her, but it wouldn't matter if she got away. They were about a third the way across the bridge when he saw the two homeless men walking towards them from the other side. When they noticed the girl they broke into a run as well. It was just a feeling in his gut, but when Erroneous saw them he knew that these men were part of Bella's murder. He also realized he was now on a bridge running full speed towards murderers that probably had guns.

He was closing on the girl, so instead of stopping he pushed himself harder. They weren't quite half way across when he was able to reach out and grab the back of her coat. He felt a surge of triumph as his hand closed on the old brown fabric, but it was short lived. As soon as he pulled the girl slipped her slight frame out of the sleeves without even slowing.

Erroneous was left standing in the middle of the bridge, her coat hanging from his hand. The other men were only a hundred feet

128

away. Erroneous watched as they came together and exchanged words. A moment later the two men started walking towards him while the girl hung back.

"Hey fucker! What are doing?" One of the men shouted at him.

Erroneous didn't respond. His thoughts were a whirlwind of fear and contradiction. He knew somewhere deep inside that the three people in front of him were responsible for Bella's murder. He just didn't know what to do about it. He wasn't a character from one of Dante's Kung Fu movies and these guys probably had a gun anyway. Still he couldn't bring himself to run away.

"Shithead! I'm talking to you." The man shouted again.

As they got closer Erroneous could tell they were younger than he initially thought. Not as young as the girl, but still young men. They reminded him of some of the people that would come by his father's place when he was a child. He could see how drugs and life on the street had worn on them. It gave a layer of agedness to their features that was out of place.

"Give back the jacket before we fuck you up!" The other man shouted, both arms hung loose at his sides but his eyes were open almost impossibly wide.

The threat snapped Erroneous out of his frozen state and he began to slowly walk backwards away from the approaching men. The jacket felt heavy in his hands but he didn't let go of it. He couldn't. Bella's ring might be in one of the pockets.

"Where ya going?!" The men began walking towards him faster.

They were maybe twenty feet away when one of them reached inside his coat. The man pulled something out. Erroneous couldn't see it, but he knew it was a gun. He turned and ran.

Instantly everything was panic. He could hear them shouting at his back as they began to chase him back across the bridge. Erroneous was tired and it wasn't a heartbeat before he heard the sound of their running feet catching up to him. A loud bang like a firework or car backfiring startled him so bad that he almost tripped. He looked back to see the man with the gun had stopped and was aiming at him. He could just see a whiff of smoke trailing from the end of the barrel.

There was still too much bridge left. Erroneous knew that even if he made it back across without taking a bullet, they would still probably catch him on the other side. His mind raced. It wasn't that he was scared to die. The way he felt now he almost wanted it. Erroneous just didn't want to die shot like Bella and his dad. He could accept death, but just not like that.

Before he couldn't even think about it, he took the only other available option. He stopped and turned towards the railing. It wasn't very high. Erroneous grabbed it with his free hand and in one smooth motion he swung both his feet over. There was a small twinge of satisfaction at the efficiency of the movement and then he was falling.

Erroneous had never jumped off of anything taller than a foot stool before. His stomach didn't seem to want to fall with him. It flew up into his throat, and when he opened his mouth to scream, he half expected it to fall out. The rush of cool air and burst of adrenaline swept everything clean. A crisp lucidity overtook him. Everything took on a hyper focus.

He looked out at the city as he fell and couldn't remember ever seeing it so sharp and clear. The river stretched out in front of him. The lights on the water a blurred rippling mirror of reality. He instinctively crossed his legs and wrapped his arms tight around himself. He was still clutching tightly to the coat and it trailed raggedly above him like a broken umbrella as he fell. He imagined that he must look like a failed Mary Poppins. Then in flash of sound and cold and darkness he was under water.

He didn't plunge straight down. The jacket he held seemed to catch the water like a parachute. He felt the force yank his arm hard. Pain blossomed in his shoulder but he didn't let go. The current spun him around and for a moment he didn't know which way was up.

For a few heartbeats he just sat limp in the cold smothering darkness as the river pushed him this way and that. He could stay down here he thought. He could just keep his eyes closed and let the river wash everything away. Erroneous didn't really want to die, he just wasn't sure if he wanted to live either.

The temptation to lay back and let go was strong, but as his lungs began to burn his instinct to live overpowered his dark thoughts. He began to frantically kick and flail. Just when he was sure that death was no longer a choice, his head broke the surface. A breath that was as much pain as relief filled his lungs.

Chapter 10

"To a father growing old nothing is dearer than a daughter."

–Euripides

Officer Hern Senara sat at one of the communal work computers at the station. His shift was over and he had already changed into his civvies. On the screen in front of him was an image captured from his body cam. He wished being a police officer was more like it was in the movies or TV. Then he could ask some buddy of his that worked in records to run this photo through the "database" for a hit. Unfortunately nothing in real life is like the movies and he was just staring at the face of somebody he didn't know and hoping.

He knew that the chances of seeing the guy again were slim, but he was the only person in 6 months to say he had seen Hern's daughter anywhere. He wished he had gone with his gut and followed the man. The guy didn't give Hern the willies the way some of the people he had run into did. There was just something off about him.

Most people that pass by you are on their way somewhere so they move with a kind of purpose. This guy had seemed distracted and withdrawn. Normally Hern would just chalk it up to the person being stoned or something. It happened often enough on the street, but this guy seemed completely sober.

He couldn't place his finger on it, but he could just feel something wasn't right. That combined with the guy saying he had seen Tanda, and Hern knew it would bother him all night. He hadn't planned on going home right after work anyway. Ever since Tanda left, the house was empty.

He and Angel would take turns staying with each other at their different places on the weekends, but during the week they both had to be at work too early. They had discussed moving in together, but Angel said they should wait until he wasn't dealing with so much. She was right, he didn't want to use her as a crutch or even worse a target for his depression. Angel had been a blessing after his daughter Perdita died. It wouldn't be fair to her, no matter how lonely he felt sometimes.

All Hern Sanara had wanted to do since becoming a father was take care of his family. It was why he had decided not to reenlist in the Marines and joined the Portland Police Bureau. He didn't want to be on the other side of the world while his children were growing up.

It had been hard when his wife died, but when he failed to protect Perdita he almost followed after her. Talking with Angel was what had kept him back from the edge. That and Tanda. He knew that he had failed her just as much as he had failed Perdita. He had been too selfish and caught up in his own pain. He had been so focused on what he lost that he didn't take care of what he still had. Now Tanda was gone too. She was out there and he couldn't protect her. All that mattered was finding her before it was too late.

He was trying to decide if he was going to spend his evening back on Hawthorne or driving up and down 122nd, when someone walking up behind him pulled his attention away.

"Staying late to crack a big case?" Hern heard a voice say behind him and felt a hand come down on his shoulder.

He looked up to see Sergeant Conroy leaning in over his shoulder to look at the photo on the screen. Conroy was still in his uniform. The radio clipped to his collar squawked in Hern's ear. Hern shrugged him off his shoulder and turned slightly to face him.

"Yeah, right." Hern responded. "Just looking into a lead on Tanda."

Hern and Conroy had come onto the force together. Conroy was your prototypical lifer. The kind that grew up wanting to be a cop and knew just about everything there was to know about being a cop. Conroy had advanced to Sergeant quickly while a combination of family problems and general disinterest had left Hern in basically the same place he had started. They had stayed friends despite the differences in advancement and Conroy even went out with Hern on some weekends to look for Tanda.

Conroy seemed to be studying the picture intently. "You think this guy knows where Tanda is?" He said, still without looking away from the image.

"I don't know. Maybe." Hern replied noticing that Conroy was more than a little interested in the photo of the man in front of them. "Do you know the guy or something?" He asked.

Conroy looked at the photo blankly for a few more seconds before Hern saw something like recognition light up in his eyes. "I have seen this guy before." He said. "I saw him this morning as a matter of fact." Conroy continued.

"You're kidding." Hern was skeptical and a little nervous. Conroy worked homicide and Hern wasn't sure that seeing this guy was a good thing at all.

"Don't worry, he isn't a perp." Conroy informed him giving him a little bit of relief. "There was a shooting at a diner on 122nd early this morning. Robbery gone wrong. That guy was the victim's husband." Conroy took a deep breath before resuming. "I had to tag along for the notification. Doing that is the worst. I swear I would rather be shot than notify next of kin."

"Do you have a name, address, anything you can give me?" Hern could feel his adrenaline start to rise as he asked.

"Just a sec." Conroy said pulling out his notepad and flipping through the pages. "I wrote it down because it was so weird."

When you have failed to protect what you love as epically as Hern had, even the slightest glimpse of redemption becomes everything. He had done nothing but fail as a father, husband, and protector. If he could bring Tanda home safe, he promised that he would change. He would be the father she needed and deserved. He wouldn't fail her again he promised himself over and over again.

Conroy interrupted his internal mantra. "Here it is, *Erroneous Conception Truth*." He said. "Sounds Spanish."

Hern rolled the name around his head and tongue for a few moments before it made sense, and then didn't. "Let me see that." He said holding his hand out for Conroy's notepad. "Are you sure that is his name?" He looked down dubiously at the scribble on the paper Conroy had handed him.

"Yeah. Why?" Conroy obviously hadn't made the same connection Hern had.

"Because it isn't Spanish, it is actually kind of messed up." Hern began to clarify.

"What do you mean?" Conroy asked before quietly repeating the name under his breath several times.

"ERRONEOUS CONCEPTION TRUTH." It took Hern saying it loud and slow with the proper accent before Conroy put it together.

"Does that mean what I think?" Conroy asked.

"Yep." Hern answered.

"That's fucked." Conroy stated.

"Yep." Hern confirmed.

They both just sat there for a moment processing how demented your parents had to be to name you something like that. "Do you have an address?" Hern asked, snapping out of the thought.

"Nope, but you can probably look it up pretty easy." Conroy replied. "I can pretty much guarantee that he is the only person on file with that name."

Hern just nodded at that. "I appreciate the info Conroy. Thanks a lot."

"Anytime man. Let me know if you need anything or find out anything else." Conroy patted him on the back again before walking away.

Hern typed the name into the computer and waited for it to complete its search. He wrote down the address and phone number on file. He was disturbed to see the manslaughter conviction. It wasn't murder and there didn't appear to be anything else that showed a history of violence or even real criminal activity, but it still put him far from at ease.

He knew it was possible that this guy had nothing at all to do with his daughter. He may have really just seen Tanda somewhere and happened to run into him later. Even if he discounted the man's distraction to him having, what Hern knew must be, one of the worst days of his life he still couldn't shake something else. There was something stuck in his head like a thumb tack.

This guy, Erroneous Truth, said he had seen Tanda somewhere on 122nd. Conroy had told him that this same guy's wife had been killed earlier this morning on 122nd. For Hern, that was too much to be ignored as coincidence. The possible connections sent a chill down his spine and left a twisted knot in his stomach.

Hern knew he wouldn't be able to let this go until he played it out. He picked up the handset on the desk phone and dialed the number the computer had given him. After a few rings a voicemail message began. He didn't want to explain over voicemail how he had gotten the number so he hung up.

He would try another call later and drive by the address before heading back to search Hawthorne again. It wasn't lost on him that it was where he had run into Mr. Truth. Tanda had loved the Hawthorne district. She always told him that she wanted to live there someday. It wasn't the only place around the city that he looked for her, but it was where he searched the most often. He just felt like she was close when he was there. He had hoped that the feeling was more than nostalgia, but it didn't really matter since it was all he had, until now.

He picked up the phone and dialed again. "Angel Breen, how can I help you?" The voice sounded cheery, but not quite bubbly.

"It's me sweetheart." He knew he sounded tired and was once again amazed at how she could always sound so positive at the end of what he knew was always a rough day.

"Oh, hey. How has your day been?" She asked. "I can see by the number that you are still at the station."

"Yeah, but it isn't overtime." Hern explained. "I am following up on a tip about Tanda."

"No way!" She exclaimed. "That is great! Is it promising?"

Part of the reason Hern had found himself so attracted to Angel in the beginning was her ability to genuinely care about people. She had a way of finding just the right emotional volume to match whoever she was talking to. She was excited and supportive when he was excited about something and comforting and supportive when he was feeling bad about something. She was always supportive. It was support Hern had desperately needed after everything that had happened.

"I am not sure yet. It could be." He didn't really want to get into the details with her until he knew more. "I am going to do some running around tonight and see if anything comes of it."

"Okay. Be safe." She could tell he was being short, but he knew she wouldn't push. "Let me know what happens. Are we still on for dinner tomorrow?"

"Of course. I will call you in the morning." He answered.

"Okay. I love you. You can call me later tonight if you need to or feel like it." She offered.

"I will if anything comes of this. Love you too." He wasn't sure that he meant it.

They had been saying it for a month or two now, but it still felt strange to him. He wasn't sure that he didn't mean it either. It was just hard to explain. He had loved his wife so much. He had never imagined saying I love you to anyone other than her.

His wife had been gone for a long time now. Angel had been there for him when he needed somebody the most and he knew that he did love her for that. He just wanted to be sure that he loved her for her also. He took a deep breath and pushed the contemplations out of his head for now.

An hour later he was driving slowly through the Hawthorne district. He had stopped by the address and called the number again with no luck. Now he had reconciled himself to a boring night of rolling up and down streets and praying to get lucky. It was what he was going to do anyway. He could call and check the address for Mr. Truth again tomorrow and or every day after until he got ahold of him.

The static squawking of a police scanner came from his passenger seat. He always kept it on and close now, even when he was home. The chances were slim, but he listened intently to each call that came over the wire just in case it could have something to do with Tanda. It was strange to hope that you would hear your daughter's name come over the police scanner, but it is what it is. Even if it meant she had been arrested for drugs or theft, at least he would have her back. At least she would be safe and he would have another chance at everything.

He had just circled the block and was turning back onto Hawthorne for another pass when he heard a call come over the scanner that made him immediately pull to the curb. He grabbed the scanner out of the seat and turned up the volume holding it closer to his ear. The dispatcher sounded worked up. He could tell this was more than just a traffic stop.

"All units, all units. Please Respond. We have a reported 11-6 and possible 11-45 on the Hawthorne Bridge." All police radios seemed to sound like an only slightly clearer version of an adult talking in a Peanuts cartoon. "Repeat, reports of an 11-6 and possible 11-45 on Hawthorne Bridge. All units respond."

It felt like someone taken hold of both ends of the knot in Hern's stomach gave a strong jerk. It wasn't so much like a punch as it was a wrenching. The call on the radio could be completely unrelated, but Hern could just tell that today wasn't that kind of day. He pulled out into traffic, cutting off some smart car, which earned him a dinky little honk and a waving finger in his rear view.

He wasn't sure what he would find or do when he got there, but he knew he had to check it out. If he hit the lights right and traffic wasn't bad he could be at the bridge in 5 minutes. Hern accelerated as much as he could, weaving around cars in the road

ahead of him. He could already hear sirens in the distance and

closing fast. Something inside told him that he needed to get there

first. He lay on the horn, trying through force of will to get traffic to

open up in front of him. He pulled out his phone and tried the

number for Erroneous Truth again.

Chapter 11

"It is a strange thing, but when you are dreading something, and would give anything to slow down time, it has a disobliging habit of speeding up."

— **J.K. Rowling**

Dante was pissed. Actually Dante was really fucking pissed and more than a little scared. He had been chasing Erroneous' little dot on his phone all fucking day. He had to cancel all of his appointments and showings for the day and he was pretty sure he had lost at least one client.

He actually wasn't too upset about that. Honestly the lady was a snob and had no fucking reason to be. She had a pre-approved

USDA loan for an amount that wouldn't buy an outhouse in the current market. She insisted on seeing every house she couldn't afford and wouldn't even walk into anything actually in her price range. Dante was more than half convinced the lady was just bored and had no real intention of buying a damn thing. She was one hundred and thirty years old and probably just stoked to get out and drive around with somebody.

It had definitely been too long since he had blazed. He was letting stupid shit distract him and make him pissy when he had important shit to worry about. To say the day had been frustrating was a gross understatement. If he didn't spark a joint soon he was going to end up screaming at group of small children or punching a clown or something equally asinine.

First he had missed E at the examiner's office. He had to tell the lady behind the desk that he was E's brother to even get her to do anything. Then she just called a different lady that spent twenty minutes asking him if he had been in contact with his brother and informing Dante about the importance of family support in times like these. She then spent another twenty minutes lecturing him about making sure they contacted the detectives and are available to make arrangements for the body and the importance and availability of grief counseling. When he finally thought she was done, she asked him to wait while she gathered up some paperwork for him to fill out and found some resources for him to take home.

Dante didn't wait. The lady reminded him of a slightly sadder female version of Mr. Rogers. Which meant there was a good chance she would forgive him for his rude exit and probably have all the papers neatly stacked and waiting for his or E's return. Dante envied her. People like her probably had a smoother day. He shuddered to think how much time and energy and time he wasted in a day being frustrated with people instead of just moving on. Not to mention how much extra work and drama it created.

After he left, he continued chasing after E's little dot. It had moved to the area where Dante knew Bella worked. Had worked. Dante still hadn't bothered to process that Bella was dead.

They hadn't been personally close. The only thing they really had in common was how much they cared for Erroneous. He knew what she had meant to E. He also knew that his friend was in the most pain of his life right now.

Dante loved E and it wasn't something he was ashamed to admit. It wasn't romantic. He didn't want to fuck or cuddle. He just truly deeply loved his friend more than any other person on this earth.

Dante didn't have a pair of rose colored glasses. He didn't hold stock in any great altruisms or in general give a shit about the way things should be. He faced the world in the raw and real. Dante knew and accepted that in this world all but one thing can be bought.

The one thing that can't is a true friend. To Dante that was the only real love there was. Not even family counted. So called blood ties are usually just the first people close enough to betray you.

Romantic love always faded. That is why married people are always bitching about how little sex they have. That is why most marriages don't work. The only marriages that last are rooted in a strong friendship.

When someone is a true friend, there isn't enough money or pain or fear in the world to make them turn on you. Most people never actually have a true friend. They have people they are close with and who can hold up under small amounts of pressure, but not a single person in their life that wouldn't sell them out for the right price. Dante had only ever had one.

When he was released from juvie, Erroneous was sent to a group home. He had written and Dante tracked him down after getting released and splitting from his own state assigned group home. They hopped a boxcar into Victorville after that. He had wanted to go all the way to Los Angeles, but E had pointed out how Victorville seemed much more affordable. The California High Desert may not have been the popping scene that Dante imagined L.A. offered, but it was a great place for living on the fringe of society and staying under the radar.

It hadn't taken long to find a weed connect and a place for them to crash. Malcam wasn't the worst predator out there. That being said, he was still the kind of person that would sell drugs to high school kids and let homeless minors live at his house. Sure, most people would consider Malcam a low life, but there are more people out there like Malcam than you would think.

They hang out with kids because that is their clientele. They are usually too big a piece of shit to have any adult friends that won't turn them in to the police. Kids are still too naive to know any better. Still too easily flattered by adult attention.

You can find people like Malcam in any shit hole town with a drug problem. All you have to do is find the kids that nobody gives a shit about and see where they hang out. That is where you will find people like Malcam. They are there handing out everything your parents told you stay away from. They are there murmuring to lost kids that everything will be okay, when it won't. That is all a lost child wants to hear from any adult. The drugs made it easier to believe.

To a couple of kids like Dante and Erroneous, he seemed like a savior. From young Dante's line of sight, Malcam was a fucking role model. He always had the best drugs. He always had the hottest, sluttiest, young chicks over. He was an adult so he could buy whatever he wanted and party all of the time.

Malcam let E help him grow weed. Dante would go out to the schools and make sales. All the kids treated Dante like a gangster from a movie. He was so fucking full of himself back then.

He thought he was so cool because he had money in his pocket and didn't go to school. He didn't have anyone telling him

when to come home or what he couldn't do. Even looking back now, Dante wasn't sure he would have traded it all in for a nice house with two loving parents and your perfect suburban story. Not that he could, so fuck it anyway.

Things were great for a while. The weed got better with E helping and they were selling out as fast as they could grow it. There was also plenty of meth and other shit flowing through the house, but Malcam handled most of that. Dante had all the fresh gear he could want and bitches hanging on him all of the time. Life was good.

One day Dante and Erroneous were in the living room trimming the latest crop of weed when there was a loud knock at the door. It was the kind of loud forceful knock they referred to as a "cop knock". They always knew that there was too much shit in the house to even bother hiding any of it if the cops showed up. The main plan in the case of a cop knock was to hide any cash. Dante had immediately jumped up and rushed to the back of the house to do just that, while E went to look through the peephole.

"Just a second. I'm taking a shit. I'll be right there." Dante heard E yell from the other room. His shout was interrupted by the sound of the door crashing in and windows breaking in the back bedrooms.

They had a code for when somebody knocked on the door. "You fucking guys" meant it was just regular customers and all clear, "I'm using the Restroom" meant cops, and "I'm taking a shit" meant run, run, run. Dante was in the bathroom. The cabinet under the sink had a false back that had an opening behind it about as big as the cabinet space itself. It was where they hid their money and stash. When Dante heard E shout and all of the glass breaking he panicked and crammed himself into the cubby, pulling the cabinet door shut and sliding the false back into place behind him.

Everything was muffled but he could hear multiple people moving around and yelling. It sounded like a demolition crew was moving through the house. Dante could hear furniture being thrown over and more glass breaking. At one point somebody came into the bathroom and threw everything around. They looked under the cabinet but didn't notice the false back. Dante held his breath and almost shit himself with fear.

The sacking went on for a good 20 minutes while he hid, curled into a ball in the small space. The next sounds Dante heard were far worse. He could hear a man screaming, but couldn't tell

what was being said. Whenever the man paused Dante could hear

soft thuds and the sound of Erroneous whimpering and crying out.

Dante knew they had to be trying to get E to tell them where

to find the money. He expected one of them to come back into the

bathroom at any moment. Dante hid for what seemed like forever,

until the men finally left. Erroneous didn't break and Dante had

never forgiven himself for it. After E got out of the hospital they

decided to move to Oregon.

Dante physically shook the dark memory from his head. E

had headed towards the Hawthorne District before he could catch up

and now the dot was just floating around the Hawthorne Bridge and

had been for over an hour. Unfortunately it didn't tell him if E was

on the bridge or underneath it. He had driven across the bridge once

after it looked like E was heading that way, but as soon as he got to

the other side E's little dot headed back. Dante almost lost his shit

trying to get turned around and back onto the bridge in downtown

traffic.

When he finally got back over, Erroneous' dot did it again,

and like a fucking idiot he turned around and drove back over the bridge. It had taken him an hour and a half to drive over that fucking bridge twice. By the time he drove back to the eastside for the second time he was literally having an anger seizure and cussing at people while hanging halfway out of the window. It was not his finest moment but he chalked it up to too long without a hit and desperation at his continuing inability to find and help his friend.

It didn't help that it had started raining and now was getting dark. Why was it that bad things always happened so fast, but it seemed like the whole world was in your way when you are trying to help? Dante had parked his car in the first spot he could find after getting off the bridge. He grabbed a joint from his glove department stash, lit it up, and started following the dot on foot. He was just about to hit the bridge on foot when E's dot started moving again.

"You gotta be fucking kidding me." Dante said under his breath and started walking faster. He hadn't quite hit the main span when he saw E about halfway across.

"E!" He shouted, but doubted he could be heard from where he was. "Erroneous!" He screamed.

Erroneous turned around and started running in his direction and for a second he thought E had heard his shout. Dante felt relief wash over him. He could feel a weight lift and tension leave his body in a rush at the sight of his friend alive and heading his way. The sound of the gunshot surprised him so much that he actually turned away and clenched his eyes shut. He opened them just in time to see E leap over the railing and fall towards the river.

Dante opened his mouth to scream but nothing came out. It was like he had the wind knocked out of him. The surge of panic and adrenaline came on so strong and fast at the sight that it felt like all his muscles clenched at once. He could feel his whole body burn as he tried to make himself move but didn't know what to do. He just gaped, feeling terror and bile rise up inside as he watched Erroneous fall.

The sight of E hitting the water snapped him out of it. He dropped the still burning joint and sprinted down the bridge walkway towards the river walk. He got to the water's edge just in time to hear E break the surface gasping and splashing somewhere out in the water. Tears had started to run down his face and he couldn't see his friend through the blur, but Dante dove into the cold dark water without hesitation. The shock of the water left him dazed for a second, but he just kept paddling toward the sound of his struggling friend. When he wrapped his arms around Erroneous, he was actually happy that E flailed for a second. It meant he was still alive.

"It's me. I got you brother." Dante whispered loudly in his friends ear between harsh breaths, and felt Erroneous stop struggling and try to turn his head back to see him. "I got you. It's okay E. I got you." Dante just kept repeating it as he labored his way towards the shore with Erroneous in his arms. "It's okay. I got you." He didn't know if he was saying it to reassure his friend or himself. He was still crying but he didn't care. "I got you brother. It's okay. I got you."

Chapter 12

"We think too much and feel too little. More than machinery, we

need humanity; more than cleverness, we need kindness and

gentleness. Without these qualities, life will be violent and all will be

lost."

-Charles Chaplin

Erroneous almost passed out on the way back to shore and

was barely able to pull himself out of the river onto the small dock

jutting out into the river. Dante helped drag him the rest of the way

after getting out himself. For a while all he could do was lie on his

back and breath.

Everything hurt. He still had the jacket clenched tightly in his fist. He hugged himself with his free arm clutching his wounded shoulder. The whole world seemed to be vibrating and the blood pounding in his ears drowned out everything else.

"E? You okay man?" Erroneous wasn't able to respond at first. "E? Are you alright? Come on E." He could see Dante standing above him, but everything seemed garbled.

"I'm…." He tried to push himself up, but failed.

"Fuck me running! I thought you were fucking dead!" The relief was apparent in Dante's voice as he kneeled down to help pull Erroneous into a sitting position.

"I'm okay." Erroneous croaked out right before being doubled over by a fit of coughing.

"Are you sure? Because you look like shit." Dante pressed. "What the fuck is going on E?"

"I don't know." Erroneous barely whispered after the wracking coughs subsided.

It wasn't a lie. He had no idea what was going on anymore. describing things as overwhelming was beyond comical. Erroneous felt like he was barely holding onto his sanity. He wasn't even sure he was still holding on.

"You don't know?!" He could tell Dante was freaking out. "Who was shooting on the bridge? You jumped off the FUCKING bridge!"

"They killed Bella and took her ring." Just saying it again made Erroneous feel dizzy. "I was trying to get it back."

Erroneous began to empty his pockets onto the dock. He wasn't sure why. He was just so tired and it seemed like what you do after falling in the water fully dressed. He had lost one shoe in the river so he reached down with his free hand and pulled off the other.HE followed it with both wet socks. Then like a needle puncturing his brain Erroneous suddenly remembered why he was still clutching so tightly to the jacket.

He quickly spread it out next to him and began rummaging through pockets, pulling them inside out as he went. The outside pockets were full of wet cigarettes and gift cards. He set each item carefully down so he didn't miss anything, but didn't find any rings.

There was something heavy in the inside pocket. Erroneous reached in and pulled out a hotel room key card and small chrome pistol. Erroneous didn't know anything about guns, but this didn't look like much of one. It didn't have to be to kill somebody he guessed.

He put the gun back into the pocket and put the wet jacket on before standing up. It was a struggle with his injured shoulder. It felt dislocated, but he had never had a dislocated shoulder before so he wasn`t sure. One thing he knew for sure was it hurt really bad.

Erroneous checked each of coat the pockets one more time. He reached his hands in deep, pushing his fingers into the corners of each pocket, but Bella's ring wasn't there. It was possible that it had been. It could have falen out in the river. Erroneous didn't believe that. He couldn't believe that.

He stared down at the key card. They had to still have the ring somewhere and now he knew where they would be. He could still do this. He hadn't failed Bella. He hadn`t lost everything yet.

"The New Days Inn." Dante said reading the card over his shoulder. "Is that theirs?"

"I d-don't know." Erroneous replied. The cold was starting to set in. "I think so."

"Then let's go E." Dante sounded stressed and confused. "Let's get out of here before the fucking cops show up. Let's go find those motherfuckers and......" Erroneous could tell that Dante was getting angrier and wanted an outlet. "And fucking....just handle it. Fuck! You know I always got you E."

Erroneous did know. He knew Dante would do anything for him, just like he would do anything his friend and brother. In the past he had seen just how far Dante would go for him. He knew Dante would always be there for him and would always be willing to sacrifice for him.

Erroneous couldn't let that happen. He knew that the people in his life felt like they needed to protect him and do things for him. He knew that they believed they had to fight for him. Erroneous understood.

It was what you did for the people that you love and Erroneous was infinitely grateful. Nothing felt better than knowing there was someone that cared enough to fight for you. It meant that much more to somebody like Erroneous. It was the rarest of things in his life and the most precious.

What they didn't always understand was that Erroneous loved them too. He could never have made it in this world without Dante fighting for him, but sometimes you have to fight your own fight. Nobody is an island, but there are moments and actions in our lives that are solely our own. Things we have to do and face alone. Decisions that are only ours to make. Fights that only we can fight.

This was Erroneous' quest. This was his fight and no one else's. He knew Dante would help, but that wasn't the point. He wasn't going to let Dante do this for him. Not this time. Erroneous needed to do this himself. It was his turn to fight for what he loved. He knew if he didn't walk through this fire he would feel like he was burning forever.

"We can't go." Erroneous said and watched Dante's expression become confused.

"What the fuck do you mean?" Dante yelled. "They killed Bella! They almost killed you!"

"I know." Erroneous had positioned himself so Dante was between him and the river. "That's why this fight is mine. I don't want you to get in trouble for it."

"Wha.." The question remained unspoken as Erroneous shoved Dante into the river.

He didn't wait to see what happened afterwards. He just ran and hoped Dante would forgive him. He would explain everything when it was over and Dante would understand. Maybe by then Erroneous would too.

"E! What the fuck! Come back here! Motherfucker!" He could hear Dante screaming and splashing behind him as he booked it barefoot towards the New Days Inn.

Erroneous made sure to take a winding indirect route. It would take longer, but it was necessary. He knew that Dante would be trying to find him. There was a chance the police were looking for him by now too. He didn`t get this far too be stopped now.

His burst of adrenaline had faded fast. It didn't take long for the fatigue of the day and the pain in his shoulder to catch up to him. It was still raining and the cold was quickly consuming what little energy Erroneous had left.

He had walked 6215 steps since pushing Dante in the river, but was unsure where he was at anymore. He didn't know when he had cut his foot. It had been so cold that he hadn't noticed at first. He noticed now. Each shuffling step shot sharp pain into his brain.

Between that and his shoulder, Erroneous felt like the world was

literally chewing him up.

It was probably the only reason he was still conscious.

Erroneous stumbled another 47 steps before the world spit. His foot

caught on a raised ridge of concrete sent him falling prone onto the

sidewalk. He was trying to remember his step count when

exhaustion finally robbed him of awareness.

***

The man wasn't paying much attention as he meandered

slowly down the sidewalk. It had been a good day. The people

getting onto the freeway had been more generous than usual and he

still had a good chunk of his disability check to drink on. He had

already put down half a fifth of good ole Evan Williams and had a

whole other bottle to warm him against the rainy night.

"Trailers for sale or rent. Rooms to let fiddy cents." His voice

was gravelly as he half sang half mumbled his way along. "Mmm..

mmm.. mmmm..mmmm... King of the road!"

Nothing warms the belly and the mood like whiskey, he thought enjoying his buzz. He continued to hum and sing as he let his faithful companion Skitz lead him along by the thick rope he held loosely in one hand. He didn't even notice when Skitz stopped to smell something on the sidewalk. He just kept walking until the leash pulled tight in his hand from behind.

"Come on Skitz." He mumbled giving the leash a little pull. "Leave it."

Skitz yanked back and continued to sniff at what appeared to be a pile of clothes in the middle of the sidewalk. The stared at the pile hard and waited for his eyes to focus. When they did he could tell that, as is often the case around Portland, the pile of clothes was actually a person. He pulled on Skitz's leash again.

"Come on." He tried again. "Leave em' be Skitz."

Skitz once again gave a stubborn tug back. He was supposed to be a trained emotional support animal, but most of the time the man felt like the dog was the unstable one. Skitz continued sniffing the passed out person's body until eventually beginning to lick the person's bare feet. The man could see a small puddle of blood there and knew the person must be hurt. He squatted down to get closer look as his dog continued to lick.

It was a man, and he looked like he had been drowned and then dumped on the sidewalk. His lips were blue and he was shivering. You ran into people passed out on the street a lot around here, but not usually like this. There were plenty of people that drank too much or did a little too much of whatever drug of choice. You could find them laying out on sidewalks all over town. This guy was different. He didn't look like he was high, he looked like something else had happened to him. Either way, he looked about ready to die.

"Hey buddy." He gently shook the man by his shoulder. "You okay?" The man on the sidewalk responded with a groan and his eyes cracked open but seemed to stare unfocused at nothing.

"You okay?" He pressed. "You need a doctor? You look real bad."

"No! No doctor! No Cops!" The man was trying to push himself up off of the sidewalk, but didn't look like he had the strength to succeed.

"Okay, okay. I get it." He adjusted his own backpack and wrapped his arms around the man's chest. "Okay. Up on three. One, two, ughp!" The man barely helped at all as he hauled him up off of the sidewalk and half fell half walked him to the closest wall and propped him against it.

"You sure you don't want an ambulance?" He asked again.

The man shook his head adamantly. "Can't.. Have to go.." He caught the man as he tried to walk off and collapsed.

"Man, you ain't going anywhere right now. Not like this. I get it. No cops, no hospital. I get it." He put the man's arm over his shoulder and started moving down the sidewalk. "At least let me help you some."

"Why?" The man mumbled.

"Why? Because I am human." He answered a little more strongly than intended. "I have lost a lot out here, but not that. I haven't lost that yet. Come on. I know a place where we can get you dry."

He continued down the sidewalk with the man leaning heavily on him and Skitz leading the way. "My name is Alex. What's yours?" He asked after a little while.

"E-Eron.. E-ron." The man barely stuttered out.

"Okay Aaron. It's okay." He said trying to sound comforting. "We are just going right up here and we can get your clothes dry and you can rest some."

There was a coin laundry on the corner. It was empty this time of night. Alex helped Aaron over to a seat in the corner. He helped Aaron out of his wet shirt and pants, then dug a blanket out of his pack to wrap him up in while his clothes were drying. The guy looked to be just a few years older than his own kid.

He always judged somebody's age based on how old his kid was. Alex had never met his kid. He didn't know if it was a boy or a girl. He had left before it was born, but he thought about his kid every day. He thought about his wife everyday too.

He knew it was better this way. Living on the streets wasn't even that bad as far as he was concerned. It wasn't any worse than living in a tent in the desert. At least here there usually wasn't somebody trying to kill you and you didn't have to kill anyone else either. He probably could get a job, even with the PTSD, but what was the point?

What was there to work for? When he first came home, Alex thought he could just not think about it again. He thought it would just be in the past and he could go on with his happily ever after. His beautiful wife was pregnant and he was going to be a father. The war was over and he was home.

He had never seen anything wrong with a drink to unwind and if he needed to drink just a little more to blunt the dreams then he didn't see the harm. The first freak out wasn't so bad. Just some broken dishes and a hole in the living room wall. The second one was worse.

When the red had cleared his wife was on the ground sobbing in front of him. The wall next to her was crushed in like a body had been thrown at it. He couldn't put together what his eyes saw. The sight of the person he loved most lying there, looking up at him in terror and pain was too much. He packed his kit and left. He never came back.

He wanted to be a good father more than anything in the world, but he knew he couldn't, not the way he was now. He had joined up and gone to war because he thought it would make him a hero. He had wanted to be a hero for her and his baby. It hadn't made him a hero at all, and he knew they were better off without him.

Alex talked to Aaron while the clothes were spinning around in the big dryer. Aaron didn't really seemed interested in talking back. Alex didn't really mind. You run into a lot of people on the streets like that. Everybody wants to tell somebody to get a job, but some of these people can barely talk to another human being.

Alex talked to Aaron anyway. He introduced him to Skitz and offered him a granola bar and some whiskey. Aaron declined the whiskey but took the granola bar with quiet thank you. He seemed like a nice enough guy. Just quiet Alex surmised.

His new friend passed in and out of sleep as Alex just carried on with his one sided conversation until the dryer's buzzer sounded. He helped Aaron get dressed. Then searched through his bag until he found an extra pair of shoes. They would fit okay and were better than bare feet.

Alex unpacked a first aid kit from his pack as well and wrapped Aaron's cut foot, before helping him put on the shoes. Aaron's shoulder also looked bruised and swollen. Alex could tell that it hurt, but it was beyond the help his small box of first aid supplies could offer. He tried to dry the man's coat but Aaron clung to it defensively. Alex decided not to press and just helped drape the blanket back around him.

"There ya go." Alex tried to sound upbeat. "Dry and fed a little. Go ahead and rest up some. I'll hang out here with ya for a few hours."

Aaron just nodded and lay back into the chair and closed his eyes. After a few seconds his breathing evened out. Alex moved to a corner of the laundromat and sat down on the floor. Skitz crawled onto his lap and after a while he let himself doze a little too.

He awoke to a cry of pain and a stern unfamiliar voice. "I said you can't sleep here!"

A police officer had Aaron bent over a washer with his arm pulled behind his back. Alex could see Aaron's face twisted in pain. Another officer was walking over to where he sat on the floor. Skitz was already out of his lap with his lips curled up over his teeth and his eyes fixed on the approaching cop.

"Hey man! Leave him alone!" Alex yelled at the police as he stood up from the floor. "He's hurt. He was just resting for a second."

"Just calm down." The officer walking toward him said reaching out with one hand to grab him by the arm.

"Fuck you! Don't touch me!" Alex yanked his arm away. "Hey leave him alone! He's hurt! We didn't do anything wrong!" He continued to yell at the officer struggling with Aaron.

Skitz had started growling menacingly next to him. When the officer tried to grab his arm again the dog attacked. His jaws latched strongly onto the cop's arm and he began to shake his head furiously back and forth. The officer cried out as he was jerked roughly to and fro.

When his partner saw what was going on he let go of Erroneous and reached for his taser. Skitz released the cop's arm and fell to the ground yelping when he was hit with the 50,000 volts. Alex saw his best friend laying on the ground convulsing under the continued shocks. The next thing he saw was red.

Chapter 13

"Most of the important things in the world have been accomplished

by people who have kept on trying when there seemed to be no hope

at all."

—Dale Carnegie

Dante sloshed his way down the sidewalk. He had barely

gotten away from the riverbank before boats started showing up in

the water with big searchlights. The main span was covered with red

and blue flashing lights and traffic had backed up for blocks on both

sides of the bridge. He was still fuming about E pushing him back into the river. Dante wasn't sure how much more of today he could take. It didn't help knowing that it wasn't over yet.

He couldn't imagine what Erroneous must be feeling and thinking, but he did kind of understand his actions. It was what Dante would have done if their roles had been reversed. He appreciated his friend's desire to protect him, but it didn't make it any easier to swallow. It also didn't mean that he was just going to give up and go home.

He knew where E was heading and he planned on being there to help. He had gathered up E's phone and wallet from the dock and shoved them into the shoe E had left behind. Then he started for where he parked his car. Dante didn't want to be discovered by one of the search parties standing on the bank of the river, soaking wet.

He was surprised to look down and see the inside of the shoe glowing. It took him a moment to realize it was E's phone. He wasn't surprised that the phone still worked after E's jump into the river. A couple years back Dante had dropped his phone into the toilet. Once E discovered that 1 in 5 people dropped their phone in the toilet, he had ordered them all waterproof cases. He had actually ordered everyone 2 waterproof cases, because even if the case saved the phone, it had still been dropped in the toilet.

By the time Dante pulled the phone out it had stopped ringing. The screen registered 23 missed calls. He knew several of those were his. There was no doubt in Dante's mind that he would forgive E. He just might have to kick his ass first. He was about to put the phone back into the shoe when it lit up again with an incoming call.

"Hello?" Dante answered. He didn't want to miss it just in case it was E.

"Hello? Mr. Truth?" Dante didn't recognize the voice and it didn't sound calm.

"Who's asking?" Dante countered.

"Sorry. This is officer Senara. We spoke earlier about my daughter." The man replied. "Am I speaking with Erroneous Truth? It is important that I speak with Mr. Truth."

Dante's mind immediately went to the girl on the bridge that E was looking for. He knew there was a chance this phone call was about somebody else entirely, but with the way today had gone he also knew he should assume the worst case scenario. What the fuck had E gotten himself into? This had to be the clusterfuck of all clusterfucks. Now the real question was whether or not this cop was going to be part of the solution or if he was just going to fuck things up more.

"Hello?" The voice on the line prompted. "Do I have the right number?"

"Shit. This isn't "Mr. Truth", but you do probably have the right number." Dante finally responded.

"What do you mean? Who is this?"

"Not yet. I have to ask you something first."

"What? What is it?" The man was starting to sound frayed.

"Are you a cop today or a father?" Dante asked.

"What does that have to do with anything?" Officer Senara returned.

"Well most days I sell homes, but today more than anything else I am a friend and I have a friend out there that really needs my help." Dante explained. "If I am right than your daughter really needs your help right now too."

"And?"

""Well, I know where they both might be. I will help a father find his daughter, but I don't talk to fucking cops. Especially when my friend might be involved." Dante took a breath then continued. "So, I'll ask again. What are you today? A father or a cop?"

There was a long pause. "I'm always a father first." The answer eventually came.

"Good. Meet me on the corner of Main and 2nd by the Hawthorne Bridge. I'll be waving a shoe over my head." Dante looked down at his soaked clothes. "We'll take your car."

Dante was shivering and in an even worse humor by the time he had walked the few blocks to the designated meeting place. He was grateful that he only had to wave E's shoe over his head like an idiot for a couple minutes before a tan ford focus pulled up along the curb. The man inside looked very hesitant. For a brief moment Dante thought he would drive off.

"Officer Senara?" Dante asked when the window rolled down.

"Not today." The man sitting in the car responded. "Today I am just Hern. Now get in and tell me what the hell is going on."

"Fair enough." Dante said as he opened the door and hopped into the passenger seat.

"What happened to you?" Hern asked staring at Dante's soaked clothes as they dripped onto the seat and floor.

"Just a refreshing evening swim." Dante replied reaching to the controls on the dash and turning the heat to full.

"The bridge?" Hern pressed.

"That was E. I just jumped in the river to pull him out." Dante told Hern. "Then he pushed me back in and ran off."

"I thought you said that you knew where he was?" Hern sounded skeptical now.

"I do. Or at least I know where he is going and your daughter should be there too." Dante assured him.

"I am not sure I like how this all sounds. What is going on? What is happening?" Hern was starting to sound more panicked than worried and Dante couldn't exactly blame him.

"I don't know if I have the answer to that question, but I will tell you what I can." Dante tried to sound reassuring, but knew he was probably failing.

"Do you know where The New Days Inn is at?"

"Yes." Hern answered.

"Start heading there and I will talk on the way." Dante instructed.

Dante gave Hern what little info he had along with his possible theories. He was not comforted to learn that Hern's information had led him to some of the same possibilities. They drove city streets just in case there was a chance of spotting E along the way, but had no luck. Dante really wished E had taken his fucking phone so he could still track him somehow.

"Which room?" Hern asked as they pulled into the parking lot.

"I don't know." Dante answered honestly.

"What do you mean?"

"I just saw the place not the room." Dante clarified.

"Then what do we do? Kick down every door?" Hern asked.

"Can you do that without a warrant?" Dante asked back.

"No."

"Then I guess we wait and watch." Dante stated. "E was on foot so we definitely beat him here. We just park and wait for him to show up."

"Great plan." Hern sounded nonplussed.

"Have a better one?" Dante retorted.

"No"

"Didn't fucking think so." Dante finished in a satisfied tone.

Hern parked the car in a spot that gave them a view of the entire front of the motel. Dante still wasn't sure if he had made the right decision bringing him here. Having a cop along could be handy if things went really sideways. It could also make things way worse. He was trying to stay calm, but it felt like he was in a nightmare and couldn't wake up.

"So this must be what a stake out feels like." Dante said trying to break the tension a little.

"I wouldn't know. Not all cops are on TV." Hern replied dead pan.

Hern grabbed what looked like big walkie-talkie off of the seat and switched it on. "This way if someone picks up your friend on the way here we will know about it." Hern explained to Dante.

"Let's hope they don't." Dante replied taking a deep breath and settling further into his seat.

"Right." Hern added crossing his arms and following suit.

Dante didn't know how long they had been sitting. A few people had come and gone from rooms since they had arrived, but nobody they recognized. The only talking had come from the radio and Dante couldn't understand a fucking word of it. Both he and Hern had just been sitting there silently watching the front of the motel.

The boredom was getting to him and it was hard to keep his eyes open. He wondered how Hern would react if he sparked a joint. Then he remembered that his stash was still in his car. It could be worse. His weed could have been in his pocket when he jumped in the river.

Dante felt just about ready to doze when a call came over the scanner that had Hern scrambling to grab it up. Dante watched Hern turn up the volume and hold the scanner closer to his ear. He could feel his anxiety rise like bile in his throat. This shit was going to give him a heart attack.

"What is it? What the fuck are they saying?" Dante started shooting questions at Hern.

"Just a second. Let me listen." Hern replied signaling Dante to be quiet with one hand.

Dante waited for only a second before pressing. "Well? What is it?"

"There are some officers requesting back up. I guess some guy attacked them when they were trying to talk to him." Hern informed Dante.

"Do you think it is E?"

"I don't know. Could be."

"How far?"

"Not far. Want to drive by and check it out?" Hern asked.

"Fuck. I don't know. I guess if it isn't far." Dante wasn't certain. If it wasn't E they were risking missing him if they left. If it was then they needed to know.

"Okay. We'll check it out and come right back if it is nothing." Hern sounded just as uncertain as Dante felt.

The officers still had their suspect sitting on the curb when Dante and Hern drove by. It wasn't Erroneous. Dante was both relieved that E wasn't sitting there in handcuffs and even more worried that his friend was still out there. He did however get a brief thrill out of watching the cops try to wrestle with a dog that looked completely crazed.

"So we head back and wait some more?" Dante asked Hern after they had passed.

"Unless you have thought of a better plan." Hern replied.

"Nope." Dante confirmed. "How long are we going to sit there?"

"As long as it takes." Hern answered.

Dante immediately noticed the door partially open to room 23 when they pulled back into the parking lot of The New Days Inn. With one glance he could tell that Hern had noticed it too. Even from this far away he could tell that the door frame was broken. Dante wasn't sure if the lights had been on in that room before they had left but they were now. He could tell by the shadows that at least one person was moving around inside.

"You noticed it too?" Herb asked turning towards him.

"Yes." Dante replied hesitantly.

"Do you think it is him?"

"What are the chances somebody else showed up here tonight and kicked a door in?" Dante replied with only a little sarcasm in his voice.

"Right." Hern said flatly pulling out his phone and beginning to dial.

Dante reached out and pushed Hern's phone down. "What the fuck are you doing?" He asked.

"I'm calling this in." Hern replied.

"What? Why?" All the ways this could go to shit had been running through Dante's head for the last few hours and most of them started with those words.

"Honestly? Because I am way out of my element here." Hern seemed ready to break. "All I know about your friend is that he has a criminal record for manslaughter and he may be in there with my daughter right now!"

"Ok. Ok. Just wait a second." Dante understood where the man was coming from, but knew that once the cops showed up things would happen too fast to stop. "Just think for second."

Hern paused and Dante took the opportunity to continue. "Right now we are just a couple of guys trying to help the people we care about." Hern seemed to be listening so Dante pressed on. "We don't know what is going on, but we know it could be really fucking bad. Right now the story is still in our hands, but as soon as you call your cop buddies it isn't."

"Your point?" Hern asked.

"Your daughter may be an accessory to murder or worse. Do you want to put her fate in the hands of the Portland Police Bureau before you know?" Dante asked.

"Good point." Hern replied "But before I listen to you I need you to answer a question for me."

"What?" Dante asked. He knew things could go either way at this moment.

"Why are you friends with Erroneous? Why are you going through so much to help him?" Dante could tell that a lot hinged on what he told Hern next.

"Have you ever met somebody that has never wanted to hurt anyone?" Dante could tell by the look on Hern's face what his answer was. "Me either, except for E. People have been stomping on him his whole life, but he keeps getting up." Dante wasn't sure where he was going with this, but he pressed on anyway. "E's the smartest person I know, but he isn't good with people. Why should he be? He has never really cared about being rich or famous. He doesn't spend all day thinking about how great he is or being mad

that someone didn't notice him. He's not as shitty and petty as the

rest of us and everyone has always attacked him for it." Dante could

see that Hern was listening now. "People use their life as an excuse

to be some of the worst assholes around, myself included, but not E.

He has faced the worst this life can throw at him and was strong

enough to not be ruined." Dante didn't know what else to say "E has

never let me down and I am not letting him down today."

"I understand." Was all Hern said in reply before tossing his

phone on the dashboard in front of him and opening up his car door.

"What are we going to do?" Dante asked opening his own

door and stepping out.

Hern pulled a gun out of a holster tucked into his waistband

and checked the clip. "Whatever we have to do to help the people we

love." Hern answered and began striding purposefully towards the

slightly ajar door of room 23.

Chapter 14

"The Edge... There is no honest way to explain it because the only

people who really know where it is are the ones who have gone

over."

— Hunter S. Thompson

Erroneous felt like a coward running away, but when Alex

jumped on those cops he didn't know what else to do. Erroneous

really hoped Alex would be alright, but he had to finish this. The rest

and being dry had helped a lot. He still felt like he had been shoved

in a barrel and thrown down a mountain, but at least he wasn't

passed out bleeding on the sidewalk anymore.

He had been closer to the motel than he had thought. He

hoped they were still here. Erroneous pulled out the room key. The

New Days Inn was printed in gold lettering on one side. Room 23 was stamped in bold red on the other. He put it back into the jacket pocket and pulled out the pistol.

It felt awkward in his hand. It wasn't like the big handguns you see in the movies. It seemed too small, like a solid metal toy that didn't quite fill his palm. He understood how people could forget that it so easily took life. The image of holding the barrel against his own head and pulling the trigger burst into his mind like a flash bomb. He had the overwhelming desire to just not hurt this bad anymore, to not need any answers, to not need anything anymore.

Erroneous wasn't sure if it was strength or weakness that held him steady through the onslaught. He took a slow, deep breath as the feeling passed and his vision came back into focus.

He realized that he was just standing in the middle of the hotel parking lot staring at the gun. Another deep breath, slow in and hard out. He looked up, scanning the long row of doors, found the one with a 23 on it and began walking forcefully toward it once again.

A few steps away he rushed forward and kicked the door as hard as he could. He imagined that he would have to do it a couple times, but the cheap motel door flew open so easily that his momentum carried him two steps into the room before he stopped. He expected people to jump up, startled and confused by the sudden and violent entry. To his surprise nobody in the room so much as stirred. He was completely unprepared for the deadness of the space.

Most of the room was filled by a bed and a still form lay sprawled upon it. The only light came from the crack under the bathroom door at the far side of the room. As Erroneous scanned the room he saw another body occupying a chair next to a small table in the corner on his left. The body looked completely relaxed and lay more on the ground than in the chair.

As his eyes adjusted to the gloom he could see that both people were men and even in the dark he could tell that it had been a long time since either had seen a brush or soap. He recognized them from the bridge. The air felt thick on his skin and heavy when he breathed. The smell of unwashed body mixed with dust and stale smoke. Erroneous had experienced worse odors but there was something emotional about this smell. It was worse than the smell of rotting death. It was the smell of rotting life and he felt his soul cringe from it.

The bed was closest to him and he spent a long moment just staring at the person collapsed across it before his purpose for being there coalesced again in his mind. Neither man had so much as stirred since he had come crashing through the door. He noticed a couple dirty overstuffed backpacks laying half-hazard in the middle of the floor between the bed and small dresser that the held the TV across from it. Trying to keep his eyes on both passed out men, he unzipped all the pockets on each bag and shook the contents out onto the floor. It just looked like a pile of trash.

Small dirty plastic bags and pieces of used tissue were littered among dirty socks. Erroneous kicked through it gently spreading the rubbish out across the motel room floor. He opened up the small zipper bags he found amongst the clutter but only found more small empty drug bags, some unwound paper clips, a couple syringes, and a broken and charred glass tube.

He quietly crept around the room checking the tops of the tables and the dresser. He found more little baggies on nearly every surface. Each contained white powder and on the tables closest to each passed out man there was also a spoon, lighter, and syringe. The recently used accoutrement of hardcore drug addicts.

Other than a few empty Pabst cans and a couple ashtrays filled to overflowing with butts, there was nothing else in the room to go through besides the passed out bodies. He knew that they probably had the ring in one of their pockets, if they hadn't sold it yet. Erroneous could feel his dread building at the thought of having to take it from them. They had guns and unlike Erroneous, they had actually used them before.

He spent another long moment standing in the dark smelly motel room thinking about his next steps. Erroneous scanned the room again and noticed that the door was still standing wide open from when he kicked it in. He walked over and closed it. The jam was busted so it hung loosely on its hinges not quite all the way closed but not open anymore either. He should have just used the key.

He reached over and flipped the switch next to the door and a dusty standing lamp in the corner bathed the room in a dim almost sickly yellow light. While not incredibly bright the difference of going from dark to light was almost like waking up. Erroneous found himself looking around the room as if he had just entered. He wasn't sure if the light made the scene more ominous or less.

The transition was jarring. Just a moment earlier, in the dark, everything had felt unreal, like a dream. Maybe it was the details that the light brought out but everything seemed much more solid. He could see the passed out faces of the men in the room with almost surreal clarity. Each had the small angry open sores of someone that constantly picks at their skin and were smudged with dirt. The realness made the whole thing scarier he decided. Erroneous could feel the energetic pressure of anxiety begin to boil faster in his chest and stomach.

Even with the light on neither man stirred. Erroneous spent a long minute contemplating digging through their pockets while they were still knocked out, but couldn't bring himself to do it. He kept picturing himself getting stabbed by a needle as he reached in or being grabbed suddenly by one of them if they woke up. He decided to wake them up instead.

He leaned over the man on the bed and poked him in the shoulder with the barrel of the .380. "Wake up." The words made almost no sound as they cracked out of his throat.

He couldn't remember the last time he had drank anything and he had been so deep in his own mind that he somehow expected

any sound he made to be a shout. The man didn't move at all.
Erroneous wasn't sure he could find the strength or courage to yell
louder so instead he grabbed the man by one dirty pant leg and
pulled him off of the bed. The man didn't make any move to catch
himself as his head cleared the last of the mattress and dropped
immediately to bounce off of the floor. The impact did the trick and
elicited a long groan as the man began to roll over.

Erroneous heard the smelly pile of human mumble "Whass
going on?" in a slurring drowsy voice.

"Where's the ring?" Erroneous barely whispered.

"Wha? Who are you? Wha' are you.."

"Where's the ring!" Erroneous asked with more force,
cutting the man off. He had rolled over onto his back and was
rubbing his face with his hands.

"Wha ring? I don have a ring? Whatta you doin here?" The
man asked back.

The man's eyes were barely open. Erroneous could only see
white through the dark slits. The man appeared to try and look up at
him, but his head was too heavy. It bobbled up and down at the end
of his neck a couple times before settling back onto the ground.

Erroneous could feel the edges of his vision begin to blur. There was something building inside him like a wave. "The ring! You know what ring! Did you sell it? Did you trade it for all these fucking drugs? Where is it?" He was practically shouting now. The crack in his voice gave his words an edge of desperation that Erroneous absolutely felt.

He could feel himself unraveling, but not in the relaxed way that loose things unravel. He could feel the strands that held himself together fraying and snapping. They spun off with loud pings and whines like a woven steel cable failing under too much stress. Each release sending a reverberating shock through his being.

No comforting fact was found in the frantic pace of his mind. There was nothing that could make what had happened or what was happening any smaller. No routine or illusion could distract from the raw agony tearing through Erroneous. He could feel himself being peeled away.

The man just stared in confusion. Erroneous couldn't tell if it was honest, a deception, or just the drugs. The blurriness seemed to take up most of his vision now focusing his world down to a pinhole. His breathing came fast and harsh. The cable snapped and the wave building inside crashed. He grabbed an alarm clock from a bedside table and threw it hard at the head of the other, still passed out, man in the chair.

"Where's the ring?! You killed her and took it! Where is it?!" He was screaming now at the top of his lungs and waving the gun back and forth between the two men. The one from the bed just lay there and the other was curled into the fetal position. He grabbed the man he had hit with the alarm clock by the jacket and held the gun to his head.

"You killed her!!!" He screamed directly into the man's face. "I will kill you!!! Where is the ring?!!"

The man was crying and the air in the room became more pungent as he pissed himself. "We don't know man. We didn't mean…. We didn't take a ring man." Snot was running out of his nose as his sobs became more desperate. "Don't kill me. We didn't do it."

Erroneous stood up and took a step back. He could feel himself trembling as he leveled the gun at the man's head.

***

Tanda woke up to the sound of shouts from the other room and the smell of her own shit. Sometimes you just took off that hard. The stuff they got must be laced with fen. Her eyelids felt like they weighed a hundred pounds. She wasn't sure if she actually lifted them or if her bottom eyelid just fell down, but eventually a crack opened and light blazed in.

The blinding haze slowly transformed into an aged linoleum floor cover with a thin puddle of puke leading to the base of a toilet. That shit must really have some kick. Too bad she couldn't remember her peak. For the briefest of seconds the fear of overdosing vibrated her to the core. She pushed it away with self-disgust.

It took a long time to push herself up from the floor, at least it felt that way. She leveraged herself on the toilet until she was able to pull herself into a mostly standing position. Staying that way required her to lean heavily on the sink. Everything still felt like it was underwater. She stared at her reflection in the bathroom mirror. She didn't recognize the person there, but she knew what that person was.

The girl in the mirror was a murderer. She had killed her mother and her sister. She had killed two people just today. She would probably kill the baby in her belly.

She could see the faces of each person she had killed, but the woman from this morning was the most vivid. She had watch the light leave her eyes. The moment replayed over and over again in her mind. The woman had beautiful, but it had been more than just how she looked. Tanda could tell that it was the woman's life that had made her beautiful. She knew that because one moment the woman was beautiful and then the breath left her and it was gone.

Tanda wasn't even supposed to have been there. She was supposed to be on the corner watching for pigs, but the fuckups were taking too long. When she walked into the diner the lady had been digging in her purse. Tanda knew she was going to pull out her phone and call the cops or worse, pull out a gun. Tanda's mom had always carried a gun. She called it "Just in Case". Tanda had stolen it when she ran away. She pulled it out.

Tanda needed this money. This lady was about to fuck it all up. It had been so easy to pull the trigger. Tanda hadn't even realized she had done it at first. The sound had surprised her. The force had left her hand numb. Her hand still felt numb. Everything still felt numb.

The yelling from the other room intensified and dragged Tanda away from her dark reflections. She wondered what Cam and Jip were yelling about. Part of her knew something wasn't right, but was too fucked up to grasp why. She just wished they would stop, she wished it would all stop. When she opened the door and saw the ghost of the man she had killed on the bridge standing in the room with a gun she thought her wish had been granted.

He looked different than she remembered. His eyes looked wild and his clothes were disheveled. It was probably because he was a ghost now. He was standing there with a gun in his hand. It was a spirit of vengeance finally come to punish her for what she had done. She was ready.

"It was me! I killed her!" Tanda shouted at the man while tearing at her clothes. "Please kill me! I killed them all!" She was naked now except for her socks. She looked down at herself and the sight of her dirty swollen belly and what it meant locked her gaze. "I'm ready. I don't want anyone else to die because of me." Her body was shaking with tears and grief as she looked up and met the wild eyes of the ghost.

***

Erroneous was barely holding on to reality. The image of the young pregnant homeless girl in front of him was almost more than his tortured mind could take. She mirrored his pain. His eyes saw the drug ravaged face and dirty naked swollen belly. He heard what the girl had said. He knew what she meant.

He turned the gun towards her, but for a moment she was Bella, pregnant with the life he had hoped to one day give her. Then she was once again just a broken child carrying hope. A ragged whimper involuntarily tore itself from his throat. Erroneous let his arm fall to his side and let the gun drop to the floor.

He didn't know how he had ended up here, but he knew it was over. He saw realization dawn in the girl's eyes. The weight of life seemed to crush her. He watched her sink to the ground and wrap her arms around herself. She didn't have the ring. Bella was gone. He had to let her go. He knew how the crying girl felt.

Erroneous pulled the blanket off of the bed and wrapped it around the weeping child. He walked over to the room phone, picked up the handset and dialed 911. There are over 240 million 911 calls made each year. He waited for an operator to answer then set the handset down on the dresser and walked out of the room. It was what Bella would have wanted.

He looked up as he walked out the door and immediately noticed two men walking across the parking lot towards him. The first was the police officer from the corner on Hawthorne, but in regular clothes, and just behind him was Dante. As they continued towards him Erroneous saw the officer's eyes widen as his gaze traveled to the open door behind him. When the officer raised his arm, Erroneous could see that there was a gun pointing at him. He watched a look of panic emerge on Dante's face. He could tell by the look in the cop's eyes that he was going to pull the trigger.

Erroneous closed his eyes. He hoped Dante wouldn't be too upset. He let out a deep breath. When he heard the shot he clenched his eyes closed tighter and prepared himself to join Bella.

Chapter 15

"Life is full of grief, to exactly the degree we allow ourselves to love

other people."

— Orson Scott Card

Cam couldn't make sense of what was going on. The man standing in front of him was supposed to be dead. Cam had watched him jump off of the bridge. He remembered. The man had been scared of him. Cam had been proud.

He didn't know what he should do now. He wished he was smarter. Jip was the smart one. Jip should know what to do, but Jip was just lying there. While the man was yelling Jip had started shaking. Now he was just lying there. His face was pale and he had frothy spit all around his mouth. Cam had seen people like that before and he knew it was bad.

He didn't know if Jip was dead and that scared him. Jip was his only friend. He wasn't a good friend, but he was the only one Cam had. He had been with Jip for a long time, since right after he had ended up on the streets. His mom had told him that he had to leave after she caught him stealing her pills.

She needed her pills more than a retarded thief. At least that is what she had told him. So he had stolen the rest of her pills and ran away. At first he was going to look for his dad. His mother told him that the war had made him a monster. She told him that his father had hurt her when he was in her belly and that was why she needed the pills. She told him that was why he was so stupid.

Cam was going to find him and kill him. He would kill him for hurting his mom and for making him stupid. He would kill him and then his mom would love him and he could go home again. Jip was going to help him. That was what he had told Cam, but that was a long time ago.

Once Cam's pill stash had run out, Jip wasn't as nice to him anymore. Cam knew that it was only because he was sober. Once they scored again, Jip was always nicer. Jip had even let him have a gun too. It was a revolver and it made him look like Dirty Harry.

Cam didn't know who Dirty Harry was, but Jip made him sound really cool.

They were going to use the guns to be outlaws so they could get big houses and Jip could take care Tanda and the baby. Cam was excited to be an outlaw. Especially if it would help Tanda. Cam loved Tanda. She was pretty and nicer to him than Jip. She still treated him like he was dumb, but it was okay. He was dumb.

She was crying now. The man had made her cry. He had hurt her, just like Cam's dad had hurt his mom. Cam wondered if he had hurt the baby too, like his father had hurt him. It made him angry. The man had made him pee too. He had made him pee on himself in front of Tanda. She would never love him now.

He had never killed his dad, because he had never found him. This man was right here. He could kill this man. Cam would kill him for what he had done to him. He would kill him for what he had done to Tanda and then maybe she would love him and Cam wouldn't want to go home again. He reached into his pocket and pulled out his Dirty Harry gun. He knew it worked. Cam had shot it on the bridge. He had wanted to impress Jip.

The man was leaving. He couldn't just leave. He couldn't just leave like Cam's dad. He pushed himself up off the floor using the table and shakily walked towards the door. Once outside he saw the man walking away and pointed the revolver at his back. Cam never heard the gunshot. All of a sudden there was just nothing.

***

They were still several steps away when the motel room door swung open and Erroneous Truth slowly walked out. Hern could tell right away that the man had been through hell. It was more than the disheveled clothing and the dejected manner in which he was walking. There was an emotion to the image that you could almost touch. Hern could almost taste the pain rolling off of the man in front of him.

Movement pulled Hern's eyes to the open, motel room door behind Erroneous. A young man had stumbled into the doorway. It was obvious to Hern by the dirty clothes and overall appearance that the young man was a transient. Hern could see Tanda on the floor behind the young man. She was wrapped in a blanket. Her eyes were wide and full of tears as she witnessed what was happening in front of her. She looked distraught but okay. She was alive and that was all that mattered to Hern at the moment.

Hern's eyes widened as the young man lifted a gun and leveled it at Erroneous' back. Hern raised his own weapon and aimed. He had shot his gun thousands of times at the range. In his entire time on the force, he had never pulled it out to use on a person. There was rage in the young man's eyes like Hern had never seen before. He pulled the trigger. The young man's eyes widened and met Hern's for a moment. The rage was gone. The body folded limply to the ground.

Hern stood stunned staring at the pile of person in the doorway. Erroneous stood frozen in front of him as Dante pushed by Hern to embrace his friend. The sound of Tanda's sobs snapped him back into the moment. Hern quickly holstered his gun and ran into the room. He took his daughter into his arms and for the first time in a long time he knew everything would be okay. He had her back. That was all that mattered.

***

Dante squeezed E has hard as he could. He had to be sure this was real. He pushed his friend away at arms-length to look at his face, then clasped him close again. After a moment he felt E's arms wrap around him as well. He almost fell as his friend nearly collapsed into him. Erroneous' body trembling with tears. Dante adjusted himself to bear the weight and joined his friend in grief.

For a moment he thought he had lost him just like in the river. When Hern had raised that gun, Dante thought he was going to shoot E for sure. He felt it like electricity burning through his heart. When he saw Erroneous still standing unharmed, Dante had almost collapsed himself.

After a few moments he assisted Erroneous over to the wall and helped him sit. "I'll be right back. Don't worry. Everything will be okay now." He affirmed into Erroneous' ear before standing up and moving to check on Hern and his daughter.

Hern had lifted Tanda into his arms and was stepping over the body in the doorway. Dante helped hold him steady with one hand as he did. He tried not to look at the body. Instead he let his gaze travel across the motel room.

The floor was littered with trash and the smell of urine and shit was almost a physical thing. In a corner by the door lay another man. Dante couldn't tell if he was alive or not. He looked dead, but he couldn't bring himself to check. After everything else today, he just didn't have the strength left to take knowing.

Dante looked up to see Hern returning. "I put Tanda in the car." He informed Dante.

"What do we do now?" Dante asked.

"I have to call this in now." Hern said.

"Yeah. Right." Dante was still in shock.

"I already called them." A voice said from behind them.

Erroneous had stood up and was pointing towards the phone handset laying off the hook on the motel room dresser. Dante could just barely hear sirens somewhere in the distance. He turned towards Hern. Dante knew inside that it would come to this at some point, but had no idea what happened from here.

"Don't worry. I know what to do." Hern seemed to notice Dante's worried look and gave him a gentle pat on the shoulder as walked by to stand in front of Erroneous. "You have to get out of here."

"Why?" Erroneous asked. "This is my fault."

"No it isn't. The only blame you get today is for bringing me back to my daughter." Hern had taken E by the shoulders. "I owe you for that. Dante and I will take care of this."

Dante didn't know exactly what Hern had in mind, but all that mattered was he was letting E go. After Hern finished talking to Erroneous, Dante walked up and grabbed his friend, directing him across the parking lot towards the street. He pulled all of the cash in his wallet out and pressed it into Erroneous' hands. Then he retrieved E's phone from another pocket and handed that to him as well.

"Here take this and get out of here." He gave E one last big hug before giving him a push towards the road. "Go on. I will call you when this is done. I love you brother."

"I love you too Dante." Erroneous replied. "Thank you."

"I've always got you brother."

E nodded and turned around. Dante watched for a few seconds to make sure he kept moving. Once E was out of sight, he hurried back to Hern. The sirens were a lot closer now. They needed to get their story straight.

***

Hern knew what he had to do and it didn't take long to fill Dante in. He had told Tanda not to say anything to anybody until they had a lawyer. She was pretty traumatized and probably still more than a little high, but seemed to understand the importance of keeping quiet right now. She was still a minor so if they played this right he could protect her from the worst of what he knew was coming.

The 911 operator had still been on the line when Hern picked up the phone. She seemed panicked, but Hern explained as calmly as he could manage that he was an off duty police officer. The operator seemed to relax slightly after that and he began to outline what had happened. He told her that he had fired the shot she had heard and that there was a suspect down, possibly dead, and that another suspect appeared to be having an overdose. By this time lights had begun filling the parking lot outside of the motel room.

The sky was lightening as Hern pulled out of the parking lot of the New Days Inn. He had wanted more than anything to ride in the ambulance with Tanda, but couldn't. The detectives had kept him for hours answering the same questions over and over again. Hern knew how it worked, but by the time it was over he understood why people hated cops.

He had told them the truth. At least everything except the parts with Erroneous. He explained how Tanda had run away months ago. He told them about how Dante had seen a flyer and called him to let him know that his daughter was at the New Days Inn and that was why they had been staking the motel out. He told them that his fatherly instincts had overridden his sense and he had kicked open the door after he saw his daughter and two men enter room 23.

He described how the young man had come at him in a drug induced rage and Hern had no choice but to use his weapon. He informed them that the other young man was passed out on the floor when he had arrived and that it was probably an OD. Dante had remained mostly silent, simply nodding or agreeing with Hern's statements with as few words as possible. It was obvious he had done this before.

They had taken Hern's gun for evidence and his badge. It was standard procedure. He would get them back after the investigation was over and he was cleared for duty again. He didn't know if he wanted them back.

They tried to get him to come down to the station, but Hern insisted that he get to his daughter and promised he would write out his statement for them afterwards. They eventually released him and Dante with the instructions to remain available and informing them both that they would be in touch. The drive to drop Dante off at his car seemed to take forever, but Hern couldn't just leave him at the motel. Neither one of them spoke during the trip.

"I guess I will talk to you soon?" Dante said after stepping out of the car.

"Yeah. I guess." Hern had no idea how things would play out from here. He knew that being a cop would help. They would believe him over anybody else there that night. In another circumstance Hern might have felt wrong about that, but not now. Sometimes a father didn't have that luxury.

"Thank you." Dante told him before lightly tapping the top of the car and turning to walk away.

There wasn't really anything else to say. Hern put the car in gear and pulled away. He was lucky that he didn't get pulled over on his way to the hospital. He drove there as fast as he could and even ran at least one red light. A lot of the cops in town were still dealing with finding the body of a jumper on Hawthorne Bridge and investigating a shooting at the New Days Inn.

The weight that lifted from Hern upon reaching Tanda's bedside left him feeling light headed. To have her hand in his again meant more than he could ever explain. The new life growing inside her was still a shock. He was going to be a grandfather.

The thought was equal parts excitement and terror. It was so hard to know how to feel about anything at the moment, but that was okay. It was going to be okay. He knew she would still have to answer for what happened with Erroneous' wife, but they would deal with that as it came. For now he had another chance.

He had his baby back. This time he would be the father she deserved. More than that he would be the grandfather her baby deserved too. He felt a brief flash of fear wash over him, fear that he wouldn't be good enough again. He squeezed his daughter's hand and looked down at her belly. He let hope push the fear away. He had another chance. They both did and this time they would do better.

Chapter 16

"I hold it true, whate'er befall;

I feel it when I sorrow most;

'Tis better to have loved and lost

Than never to have loved at all."

— Alfred Lord Tennyson

Erroneous ducked his head as the line of flashing lights and sirens passed by. He half expected them to stop, but none of them did. A few seconds later an ambulance passed by him as well. For a few moments he watched the reflections red and blue lights splash across the wet pavement. Afterwards he simply continued walking down Halsey.

The fire he had felt all day had finally consumed itself. In its place Erroneous just felt a vast emptiness that threatened to swallow him whole. He didn't know where to go. He couldn't go home. Bella had been his home.

He hoped Hern and his daughter were going to be okay. He wasn't too worried. Dante was good with cops. He would know what to do.

He was still wearing Tanda's coat. It felt heavy and not because it was still wet. It felt like the jacket had soaked up the memory of the day. Erroneous shrugged it off before he collapsed under the weight of it. He left it lying on the sidewalk behind him as he continued walking.

It was still raining. It was just a drizzle now, not the heavy downpour from earlier. It had been slightly warmer with the coat on, but Erroneous welcomed the cold breeze and light rain. He tilted his head back as he walked and let it wash over his face.

He wished Bella was here. He knew he would wish that many more times in the days to come. She would never be here again. Erroneous knew where he wanted to be.

He could have taken the bus, but decided against it. He knew where he was going, but wasn't in any hurry. There was no reason to be. He was more tired than he had ever been in his entire life. Every step he took came as a surprise. As he walked he remembered. At first he tried to push the memories away, but the tide was too strong and they began to flood his mind.

He remembered the first time he heard her voice in that dim bar on Hawthorne. He recalled how she had looked then on the stage with the lights dancing around her. He remembered the first time he heard her say his name and the way it had made his heart beat faster. He remembered the way her skin felt the first time he touched her and the warmth of their first embrace.

His surroundings fell away as his life will Bella rushed through his head. The hot heavy smell of steam and lavender shampoo she always had after getting out of the shower. The way it felt to lie in her lap and watch a movie while she ran her nails lazily through his hair. The taste of her lips and sweat when they made love.

He remembered everything. The way she hated how Dante always smelled like weed. The sound of her laugh ran through his mind complete with the little snort she would occasionally give when she found something exceptionally funny. He recalled the way she would watch him and nod encouragingly from the audience every time he sang a new karaoke song. He remembered how that had made him feel like the most special star in the sky.

As Erroneous walked he re-lived every moment him and Bella had shared together. The memories didn't take away any of his pain, but they did seem to set it in place. He didn't feel better, but like aligning a broken bone, he knew that now he might begin to heal. At least he hoped he would.

When he finally looked up he was standing in front of the diner. He had been a different person in a different life last time he'd seen it. It didn't appear any different now than it was when he dropped Bella off at work for the last time. Looking at it he could almost imagine that the last 24 hours hadn't happened. He could be running in to drop off something Bella had forgotten. She would be there with her beautiful smile and thank you. Before he left she would give him a kiss and tell him that she loved him.

He could almost imagine it, but knew it wasn't true. He knew he would never see or feel any of those things again. He would never feel her hot breath on his neck or hear the words that had made his life worth living again. The world dimmed.

He wasn't sure why, but being here felt right. It felt like the right place to say goodbye. Erroneous followed the pathway up to the entrance. He pushed through the doors and let his eyes trace over every detail of the restaurant. He had never been inside before. He only ever dropped Bella off and sometimes picked her up. There were a few early risers sitting at the counter drinking coffee and an older couple at a booth eating, but other than that the place was empty.

"Mornin', take any open spot you like." A cheery looking woman in an apron said as she passed by with a pot of coffee in one hand and a plate with a slice of pie in the other. "I'll be right with you."

Her name tag read Cara, she had a pen tucked into a bun on the top of her head and earrings that looked like little slices of cherry pie. He remembered Bella talking about her. She had said that Cara was a little bit of a ditz but really sweet. Bella used to love gossiping to him about her coworkers at the end of the day. He would just listen, content with the sound of her voice.

Erroneous scanned the room again. His eyes landed on the empty booth closest to the door. He didn't know why, but he was drawn towards it. The smell of bleach and cleanser was strong as he approached the booth. He knew this was the spot. He could just feel it like a chunk of ice in his gut.

He slowly sat down and slid himself over to the middle of the red and white checkered cushion. The seat made that rubbing almost fart like sound that was nearly impossible to avoid with the plastic vinyl covers. It seemed wrong that the table should look so clean and normal after what had happened. There was nothing to confirm it, but Erroneous knew this was where Bella died. He could feel her there almost like she was sitting next to him.

He looked up to see the server walking over. There was trepidation in her eyes, but her gaze was on the table and not Erroneous. For a moment he thought she would turn away. Erroneous saw her steel herself with a breath and continue her approach.

"Can I get you started with a cup of coffee?" She asked with a forced smile.

Erroneous almost said yes, but stopped himself. Bella had always bragged about their shakes. She had insisted that he would love the peach pie one. He had never gotten the chance to try it. It

had never seemed that important. He ordered one now.

"I'll have that right up. Can I get you anything else?" Cara

asked.

Erroneous just shook his head no. She walked away in a

hurry. He didn't blame her. It had to be hard to pretend nothing had

happened. It wasn't a fair thing to ask of an employee. Erroneous

silently congratulated her on her composure, then let his thoughts

drift back over the last 24 hours.

He felt completely used up. His emotions were a sea of

numbness with the turbulent events of the day playing in the sky

above it. His mind seemed strangely quiet through the show. He

knew that random facts should be rattling through his head, a

constant buffer against the world.

There was only an echoing silence now. Erroneous didn't

have the energy for fear. Bella was gone. His world had become

infinitely smaller. There was nothing left to be afraid of.

He hadn't found the ring. Erroneous knew that it wasn't the

ring itself that was most important. It was what the ring represented.

Finding the ring was his last chance not to fail her.

Erroneous thought about all of the promises he had made to Bella over the years and how in one day they had all been broken. There were so many things you didn't realize you would miss. There were so many moments you didn't realize you had missed. A million heartbeats gone and each one a chance to have loved her harder, an opportunity to have been happier.

He wished he had told her that he loved her more. Each kiss they shared should have lasted longer. If he had known he would have spent more time in her arms and more time just admiring how beautiful she was. A mind like Erroneous' could follow the trail of lost opportunities and should-have-beens into insanity. Most of all Erroneous wished he had given her a child. He knew that was what she had wanted most.

'Uh hrmm." Cara cleared her throat to get his attention before setting the shake he had ordered on the table in front of him. "Would you like to order something to eat, or should I just bring you the check for this, Sweetheart?"

She seemed a little rushed despite the sparse crowd. Erroneous didn't blame her for wanting to be at this table as little as possible. "The check will be fine. Thank you." He responded without looking up.

Cara had already prepared the check and slid it onto the table timidly. Erroneous fished the money Dante had given him out of his pants pocket and set it on the red metallic, flecked table without counting. She took the appropriate bills out of the pile and walked away to the register. After she was gone Erroneous slowly slid the shake in front of him.

The large fluted fountain glass was rimmed with ice. An overabundance of whipped cream swirled to a crest at the peak and pushed over the edge dripping slightly down one side. It was topped by a bright red maraschino cherry with a wide straw pushing out of the cream next to it.

Erroneous gently set the straw into his mouth letting its cold surface settle onto his tongue. The smell of vanilla and peach filled his nostrils as he sucked the thick shake through the straw and into his mouth. The texture caught him unawares. Pieces of peach and graham cracker pie crust mixed with heavy vanilla ice cream.

He took another deep pull, swirling the sweet creamy concoction around his mouth with his tongue. Erroneous pulled out the straw and admired the thick layer of shake coating it before scooping a big dollop of whipped cream onto the end, sliding it into his mouth and slurping it all off. Bella was right. He really did like the shake. The thought brought a sad smile to his lips and he felt tears once again begin to fill the corners of his eyes.

"I'm sorry Bella." Erroneous whispered to himself brokenly. "I'm sorry that I didn't take better care of you. I'm sorry I couldn't protect you. I'm sorry I didn't find your ring." His tears were coming more freely now. "I'm sorry I didn't try this shake sooner so I could tell you that you were right. There are so many things I wish I had done or said. I'm so sorry Bella. I love you so much." His shoulders shook slightly with grief as he clasped his face in his palms.

"You okay sir?" Cara had returned with his change.

Erroneous sniffed loudly, wiping the tears and snot from his face. "Uhm, yes. Thank you."

She set the change on the edge of the table. Erroneous slid the coins away one at a time and brushed them from the table into his hand. He left the bills. He had often heard Bella complain about pain in the ass change tips. As he reached to put the change into his pocket he fumbled most of it onto the bench seat of the booth.

He let out a sigh of frustration as his grasping fingers pushed some of the coins into the crack where the cushions meet. He reached further, but only succeeded in forcing the coins further down. His hand was gone up to the wrist and he was about to just leave the change when the tips of his finger brushed up against something else. It was smoother and thicker than a coin.

Erroneous shoved his hand deeper into the cushion. He could tell now that it was a ring. He turned it in his fingertips blindly following its edges. He felt the metal twist into what he knew resembled a butterfly and he knew the hard edges that followed were that of a perfect sapphire.

He could remember the moment he slid it onto her finger. He and Bella had been talking about it for a while. Erroneous still couldn't help but be terrified that she would say no. It was just so hard to believe that he could be so lucky.

He would never forget Bella's words when he popped open the little velvet covered box. "Do you know what this ring is Erroneous Truth?" She asked him. He just gawked at her too afraid to answer incorrectly. "It's a promise to me. It's a promise that you will never give up." Bella placed her hand on his chin and pulled his eyes up to meet her intent gaze. "It's a promise that you won't ever quit on me or yourself. It means you will keep trying no matter what."

He and Bella had been through so much by then. Prison had been hard and getting out was almost more challenging in some ways. It had always been so hard for Erroneous to believe he deserved her. There were times that giving up sometimes seemed like the right thing. Bella never let him quit on them or himself.

"Do you promise to always keep going no matter how hard it is? Do you promise to believe in us? Do you promise to believe in yourself? Do you promise me Erroneous Truth?"

He could almost hear and feel the words now as clearly and strongly as he did then. He didn't think he really understood all of what she had been asking of him until this moment. Bella made him a better man. Being with her made him stronger and braver. She made him want to do the right thing and improve the world in some impactful way. She would want him to still be that man. He would still be that man for her.

"I promise Bella." His voice broke slightly just as it had those years ago. He cleared his throat just as he had in that moment and repeated more firmly. "I promise. I love you Bella. I will never give up."

Erroneous pulled his hand out of the seat cushions. The ring was wrapped tightly in his fist. He didn't even open his hand to look at it, he just clasped it fiercely against his chest. The edges digging into his palm were a welcome pain and only caused him to grip more firmly. Out of the window next to the booth Erroneous could see the sun just breaking over the horizon. The pink light was mixing with the hazy grey of the Portland morning. He slumped back in the seat and with a long sigh closed his eyes.

Chapter 17

"The weak can never forgive. Forgiveness is the attribute of the

strong."

— Mahatma Gandhi

Erroneous was sitting in his usual booth next to the door drinking a Peach Pie shake. It had been over a year since Bella's death. Since then he had tried every shake the diner made. There were 18 not counting some of the seasonal offerings. Peach Pie was still his favorite.

Erroneous' life had changed a lot in the last year, just as Erroneous himself had changed quite a bit. Dave had insisted that Erroneous take as much time to grieve as he needed and that his job would be there waiting if he still wanted it. It had taken a while to get back to a place where it mattered, but Erroneous eventually

accepted Dave's offer and returned to work.

He still awoke every morning before 5 a.m. and followed his

morning routine. It was harder without Bella's wake up kiss. He still

did his morning research, but did it at the diner now instead of the

work parking lot. His singing practice was sometimes awkward, but

he felt the attention of the few early morning diner patrons added a

certain extra reality to it. It made getting on the stage without Bella

easier.

Erroneous still very much enjoyed his facts and statistics

although he found their constant stream had slowed somewhat over

the last year and the playback was not quite as loud in his mind as

before. Now he would mostly find himself reciting them when he

was thinking of Bella. He didn't use them to push away the

memories of her the way he had with his fear.

He would often find himself whispering them quietly out

loud. He didn't care if people heard him anymore. He would imagine

Bella listening intently as if they were together and it dulled the pain

of the moment some. He missed her so much

Dante told him that it was creepy to hang out at the diner every day, but it made Erroneous feel closer to Bella. Sometimes Dante would even join him. He was at the counter flirting with Cara this morning while Erroneous perused the news. That was happening a lot lately. Observing his friend's efforts, he couldn't help but hope that Dante might finally settle down and find some of the happiness Erroneous had with Bella.

He and Dante had moved back in together. It had taken a while to readjust to Kung Fu movies playing all night, but it was better than living alone. He dragged Dante to karaoke every week. Erroneous would sing and imagine Bella cheering him on from one of the dimly lit bar tables by the stage where she always liked to sit.

The jingle of bells on the entrance door caused Erroneous to look up from his phone. Hern Senara was traversing the short space between the door and Erroneous' booth. It was the first time Erroneous had seen the man since that night. Dante had talked to Hern several times and had even testified about the events that seemed so much like a dream now. Erroneous gave his best effort to stay away from it completely. He just honestly hadn't wanted to think about it.

"Mind if I sit?" Hern asked as he got to the table.

Erroneous could only gesture in ascent to the empty seat across from him. He didn't trust himself to speak. Seeing Hern again brought a strength to his emotions that he didn't realize was still there. Erroneous' heart quickened and his breath sped up to match.

For a moment he was standing in a motel room illuminated wiht sickly yellow light. His blood pounded in his ears. He could almost feel the cold metal of a gun in his hand. Erroneous pushed the memory away with a deep breath and brought his eyes up to meet Hern's.

"Sorry to just show up like this." Hern started. "Dante said you would be here and I didn't know if you would agree to meet me." He trailed off and looked at Erroneous expectantly.

Still searching for words, Erroneous remained silent. He tried to play out all of the reasons Hern would have come to see him. He came up with a blank. He was still struggling to swallow the sudden and violent surge of emotion seeing Hern had elicited.

Seeing the combating emotions play across Erroneous' face, Hern started to push himself up from the booth. "I'm sorry. I don't know what I was thinking."

Erroneous reached out a hand to stay him. "No. Wait." He said finally finding his voice. "I'm sorry. It is just…" Erroneous didn't know the words to describe it so he didn't try. "Please, sit back down and tell me why you are here Officer Senara."

"Just Hern." Erroneous was corrected. "I resigned from the force. After what happened that night I just didn't know if I could do it anymore." He stared sightlessly out the window as he continued. "I just don't think I could pull my gun again. It is for the best. I can really be there for Tanda right now and that is what's most important."

Erroneous visibly winced at the sound of her name. "Sorry." Hern apologized noticing the look.

"It's okay." Erroneous reassured him. "It just still hurts. What can I do for you Hern?"

Hern took a deep breath and steadied himself before he continued. "I just wanted to thank you. That night was so crazy and I couldn't work up the courage until now. I should have done this a long time ago."

"Thank me? You covered for me with the cops. You saved my life. I didn't do anything." Erroneous said incredulously. "Other than almost lose my mind."

Hern paused for a long heavy moment before he answered the question. Erroneous could see his jaw clenching as if Hern was literally chewing on his words before he spoke them. "I guess that is what I wanted to thank you for." He said the words slowly as if he wasn't sure what would fall out of his mouth. "Everything that happened that day....everything you went through...." Hern hesitated again, but took another deep breath and pressed forward. "I lost Tanda's mother and her sister. I don't how many nights I sat awake wishing that I could point a gun at a person or thing responsible for their deaths and pull the trigger." Erroneous recognized the flash of pain he saw in Hern's eyes. He had seen it in his own often enough the last year. "You had that, but you didn't do it. I don't know if I could have done the same. You didn't break and I owe everything that is still good in my life to you for that." Hern's eyes were wet and shiny as they met Erroneous' square on.

Erroneous didn't know how to respond. He didn't feel like he deserved what Hern was giving him, but he could tell that it was important to the man so he accepted it. "I'm glad that I didn't." He felt like he should say more. "How is Tanda?" It hadn't been as hard to say her name as he thought it would be.

Hern reached into his pocket and pulled out his phone. He began swiping at the screen with one hand as he vigorously wiped wetness from his eyes. A smile lit Hern's face as he found what he was looking for on the screen, but the tears thickened and began to roll down the man's cheeks. There was an air of pride in the way he turned the phone screen towards Erroneous.

A bright cherubic face buried in pink blankets shined out at him. The baby's face was radiant with the kind of mouth wide open smile that only babies seem to feel enough joy to give. Erroneous couldn't help but smile slightly at the sight despite the tightness in his chest. His hand involuntarily reached out to caress the pudgy cheek on the screen.

"She's beautiful." Erroneous breathed.

"Her name is Bella Truth Senara." There was anxiety in Hern's voice. "Tanda said she always wanted to remember."

"She would have liked that." Erroneous assured Hern. That was just how Bella was.

235

"Tanda wanted me to tell you that she is sorry for everything that happened. She wishes she could take it all back." Hern couldn't meet Erroneous' eyes as he spoke.

Erroneous just nodded his head. He reached down into his shirt and pulled out Bella's ring. He still wore his own ring on his hand, but kept Bella's on a chain around his neck at all times. He squeezed it tight and closed his eyes trying to imagine her smell and the sound of her voice. Erroneous opened his eyes and looked again at the angel on Hern's phone.

"As much as I want to wish the same, I know Bella wouldn't have wanted that." As strange as it felt to say Erroneous knew the words were true as soon as he said them. "She would have been happy to know that her death had saved that baby. Bella wouldn't have taken that back for anything."

"Thank you Mr. Truth." Hern said letting out a rough sigh. "You don't know how much that means."

"Please, call me Ron." Erroneous felt a slight soreness in his heart as he said it. Everything reminded him of Bella. He didn't know if he would ever get used to it.

"Thank you, Ron." Hern repeated. "I, uh, better go. Please let me know if you ever need anything."

"Just promise me you will take care of those girls." Make it worth it, Erroneous finished to himself.

"I promise. You have my word." Hern affirmed reaching his hand across the table.

Erroneous shook it firmly and they shared a brief knowing nod, before Hern turned and strode out of the diner. He watched Hern through the window as he walked across the parking lot, got into his car, and drove away. Dante had been witness to the exchange from the counter. He politely excused himself from his conversation with Cara and sauntered slowly over to where Erroneous was sitting.

"What was that all about?" Dante asked.

"Healing." Erroneous replied softly.

"Do you think it ever gets better?" Dante inquired sitting down in the seat Hern had recently occupied.

"No." Erroneous was thoughtful as he spoke. "But hopefully we do. Hopefully we become better and maybe it becomes easier to bear."

Dante leaned back on the bench stretching his arms out wide along the back. He took a deep breath and let it out with a blast and shake of his head. Then he shook his arms all the way down to the fingertips and ended by lightly pounding the top of the table with the flats of his hands. To Erroneous sitting across from him it looked like he was trying to shake his feelings out of his body literally.

They sat together quietly while Erroneous finished his pie shake and continued to browse through his phone. In moments like theses his facts still helped bring him back to level. His talk with Hern had been hard. He was slurping the last bit of sweet peach and vanilla ice cream through his straw when Dante pounded the table again.

"Well, I don't know about you, but I sure could smoke a fucking bowl right now!" Dante declared boisterously.

Erroneous felt his cheeks redden slightly at the declaration. He couldn't help but have some anxiety. He was still on parole, but he hadn't made Dante throw out the plants when he moved in. His parole officer didn't do home visits anymore so Erroneous allowed the risk. Besides, he really enjoyed working with the plants regularly again and Dante really enjoyed the uptick in quality he had been missing without Erroneous' touch.

Dante continued, ignoring the embarrassed look on Erroneous' face. "Fine, I guess I will just have to smoke it all myself."

Erroneous couldn't help but laugh as he began to slide himself out of the seat. He left the money for the shake on the table. He made sure to leave exact change so that any remaining tip for Cara would be in whole bills. Then, after waiting for Dante to also extract himself from the booth, Erroneous surveyed the diner one last time before heading towards the door.

"Any new facts for the day?" Dante asked as they strolled across the parking lot. He had pulled out a joint and was trying to get it lit.

"There are over four million babies born in the United States every year." Erroneous stated almost by reflex. "Also human babies are the only primates that smile at their parents."

Erroneous could not help but grin slightly at the last fact. There was just something about it that made him happy. He was reminded of Hern's granddaughter. A glance at Dante's cheesy grin told him that it had the same effect on his friend.

"I like that one E." Dante said taking a long hit on the joint and exhaling a skunky smelling cloud of smoke. "I like that one a lot."

Epilogue

Tanda scratched at the band around her ankle. She still had to wear it for another year. It really fucking sucked, but it was better than jail. She reprimanded herself for cussing even if it was just in her head. She wanted to be a good example for the baby. Tanda looked over at her daughter, resting contentedly.

"Control your thoughts, control your actions." Her counselor was always saying.

It seemed like a small thing to worry about, but small things counted. If you worked hard on enough of the small things they would turn into big things. She had been learning through her recovery that the small steps count the most. She kind of hated the cliché "I am and addict" bit, but she had to admit that it was working. It was also court ordered and one of the few things that let her get out of the house.

She didn't really mind being cooped up all of the time. It made things easier in some ways. She still got a strong itch every once in a while. Holding Bella always seemed to help. Still Tanda took a strange comfort in knowing that, if she did break, the police would pick her up before she got a block away. Thinking about it now made her start to crave.

Tanda walked across the living room and scooped Bella up out of her bassinet. Her baby girl smiled up with those chubby little baby cheeks. She felt the urge begin to fade right away. It was magic. There wasn't any drug stronger than this love. She knew it the very first time she had looked into little Bella's tiny scrunched face.

It felt strange to be back home. Memories of her mother and sister still seemed to haunt the rooms, but they felt more comforting now than before. She was still coming to terms with her feelings. Counseling had helped, but it was the baby now in her arms that really had changed her.

If her daughter's cuteness didn't motivate her to be a better person, then her energy certainly robbed Tanda of any sleep needed to do any wrong. She circled her finger in Bella's face until the child reached out and grabbed it. Tanda smiled as the baby pulled the digit into her mouth and began to gum it with gusto.

The doorbell rang grabbing Tanda's attention away from doting on her daughter. With Bella in her arms she answered the door. The mailman waited on the porch with a package at his feet and a clipboard in hand. Tanda had to ask him to wait while she returned Bella to her rest.

After signing she took the box inside. Checking briefly to make sure Bella was still content, she took the delivery into the kitchen. Setting it down on top of the counter she pulled a knife from the block and began working it through the tape. A letter was taped on top of another box within. Tanda pulled the letter off, being careful not to tear it, and began to read.

Tanda,

I apologize for taking so long to send you this. I am not good at knowing the right thing to say, but I hope these words convey my true feelings. Your father let me see a photo of your daughter. You should know that he loves you both so very much.

She really is amazing. Bella would be proud that you named her after her. I wish you could have known her. She was also amazing.

I want you to know that I am not angry anymore. I still hurt sometimes. Sometimes I still hurt a lot, but it isn't the same and I want you to know that.

Ralph Waldo Emerson said, "For every minute you are angry, you lose sixty seconds of happiness."

I have decided that I have already lost enough happiness and that I am not giving up anymore. I think my Bella would agree with me. I know she would. She was always a better person than I was.

She made me a better person too. I feel like she still does. As much as it hurts to remember her, it helps too. It helps me remember the person she helped me be and to keep trying to be that.

I want you to know that she would forgive you. It was the kind of person she was. She would understand and she would forgive you. I forgive you too.

I want to be someone worthy of the love she gave me. I know that I need to forgive you to do that. It is the kind of man she would want me to be. It is the kind of person I want to be.

I don't know if it helps, but I hope it does. Bella always wanted to be a mother. She thought it was the most amazing thing you could do. She would have adored your little girl. She would have wanted you to be the best mother you can be.

I hope that you can be as good a mother as Bella always wanted to be someday. I know she would want me to help so know that I will be here if you need. I included a gift for the baby. I have faith that she will not need it the same way I did, but I hope she enjoys it very much anyway.

With all my forgiveness and love,

Erroneous Conception Truth

Tanda wiped the wetness away from the corner of her eyes as she folded the letter back up. She didn't know if she would ever be able to express to Mr. Truth what his letter meant, but she was determined to try. She pulled the remaining box out of the package. It took her a few minutes to pull everything out and undo all of the little twist ties. When she finished, she took the brand new Teddy Ruxpin bear and tucked it in gently next to her sleeping daughter.

Not The End,

A New Beginning

If you enjoyed this book,

Please let us know by giving it a review wherever you can.

Thank you for reading!

Also look for future works from M.C. Conner.

Coming Soon!

"Erroneous Youth."